"I thought you were gone," Dix said.

The blue of Sarah's eyes deepened, like the ocean suddenly dropping a fathom deeper, and she reached up and touched Dix's cheek. The palm was cool where tears had dried warm just a few minutes before. "Not yet," Sarah said.

She kissed her. Soft. Their lips barely touched, but they held them still together for a long beat. Hesitating. Like the turn of the tide, Dix thought. She cupped her hand at the bend of Sarah's waist and pulled her tight, away from the wall. Their hips nestled into each other. Dix felt the soft scratch of hair as their legs intertwined, the heat. Wet.

Dix bit Sarah's lip then kissed her hard, deep. As so often, she felt a vibration somewhere deeper than her heart, in some darker place, like an engine gunning, an animal in a den, growling, or purring. She shivered, gave in to it, and let Sarah pull her back into the room.

Getting to the Point

Teresa Stores

The Naiad Press, Inc.
1995

Printed in the United States of America on acid-free paper
First Edition

Edited by Katherine V. Forrest
Cover design by Bonnie Liss (Phoenix Graphics)
Typeset by Sandi Stancil

Library of Congress Cataloging-in-Publication Data

Stores, Teresa, 1958–
    Getting to the point / by Teresa Stores.
        p.   cm.
    ISBN 1-56280-100-7
    I. Title.
PS3569.T6486G48   1995
813'.54—dc20   94-43314
                                                                         CIP

For my mom,
who told me to go and write nice stories,
and for Susan,
who gave me the space and support to do so.

Acknowledgments

An earlier version of this novel was my thesis at Emerson College, Boston, MA. I would like to thank Chris Keane, who taught me to write plot, and my thesis committee — Ted Weesner, Eileen Farrell, and Joe Hurka — for their careful and challenging commentary and suggestions. Deirdre O'Neill and Susan Jarvis are my heartily appreciated real-world reader-critics, and Barbara Grier and Katherine Forrest have contributed invaluable editorial advice and enthusiasm.

About the Author

T. (Teresa) Stores was born and raised in North
Florida and South Georgia. She holds a B.A. in
English from the University of Colorado and an
M.F.A. from Emerson College in Boston. *Getting to
the Point* is her first novel.

I'm back at the Point. Again. I was born here ... "God's will," according to my mother, "Big Mistake," according to my father, "Just worried you'd miss somethin'," according to my grandmother. Sometimes it seems I've been getting back to the Point all my life.

Point Will, Georgia, is probably not anybody else's idea of getting anywhere, but, for me, getting back to the Point feels like trying to get somewhere. This time, anyway.

Sometimes getting back to the Point is just getting

*away from everything else. Sometimes it's running
away. The last time I was here, when Grandma died,
I was running away to the Point, and then she died,
and did I run away from the Point? Do I ever really
leave it behind?*

*That summer five years ago was important, the
summer Iris died. The Point changed then.
Everything, everyone, changed. Or maybe I changed.*

*Now I have begun to understand that summer,
that part of the Point. It is important. And now, I
have come back to the Point. This much remains the
same.*

Part One: Wednesday

It's All Downhill
From Here

Iris liked to say that you were either from Point Will or you were lost there. "Nope, you didn't ever pass through Point Will," she'd say to the stranger trying to make polite conversation. "It's at the end of the road." You had to work at polite conversation with Iris.

Dix knew her grandmother Iris's lines like a mantra. They played behind the endless summers they had spent together. While the tree frogs screamed for rain in the heaviness of after dinner,

Dix would lie on the cool cement of the front porch and watch Iris recite.

Grandma also liked to tell folks that Point Will was the second oldest city in the United States. "And a good thing, too," she'd say. "If we'd got it over St. Augustine, why we'd be stuck with those danged buses full of Yankee tourists, loudspeakers goin' on about this war and that war . . . tellin' 'em, 'this is the most beautiful street in the U.S.A.' Heck, that might've been a right pretty street before all them tour buses snagged the Spanish moss off'n the oaks." Iris's eyes would crinkle up in the corners as she warmed to her subject. "Besides, they got 'em a fort down there. Fort's good for the tourists. Who'd want to see a pulp mill?"

Iris always rooted for Florida in the Florida–Georgia game. Dix's dad, Ed, refused to watch it at his mother's house. She said, "They always hold it in Florida; it's even called the Florida–Georgia game, not the Georgia–Florida game. Georgia's not supposed to win. I wouldn't want 'em to win. Them Yankee tourists might start noticin' us."

Dix suspected that Iris didn't much give a damn about football, she just liked to rile her son. Most of the younger folks of Point Will eventually moved thirty minutes south over the state line to Jacksonville, as had Ed, and most probably felt a bit traitorous. And Iris knew just the right spots to needle. "Nope," she'd say. "Can't rightly call Florida part of the South." She'd shake her head and frown, and when she'd look down, Dix would sometimes catch the corner of her mouth curving up in a twitch. "More Yankees down there than in New York. And Miami, shoo, Miami they might as well chop off

6

and let it float on out into the Gulf. Don't nobody speak English down there no more."

Ed would shake his head slowly and draw up his thick shoulders. "Yeah, Mama, I reckon they done let Miami get out of control. Them dad-blamed politicians . . ." Then he would point his index finger (as a child, Dix had thought of it as the pointer of God) and say, "But Jacksonville's different. Most people've still got morals there. Why Brother Paul was just sayin' last Sunday night, we've got the third largest membership in the Southern Baptist Convention right there in Jacksonville."

"Twenty got saved last —" Betty would begin. But her husband would barrel on, finger dancing, "Only Atlanta and Dallas've got more. Right there in Jacksonville, Mama." Dix was always mesmerized by that dancing finger.

Iris would shake her head. "Oh, Ed," she'd always say, almost patting him on his head like a little boy, "you know it's just not the Point."

The Point is a Main Street lined with storefronts and divided by a strip of grass, moss-draped oaks, the stump of the Washington oak which died after being hit by one too many drunk drivers ("Thing was like a magnet for them," Iris said), a rusty cannon ("Not 'zackly a fort, eh?" she'd grin), and a shrimp boat dock. It is a pulp mill, twenty or so churches, and a cemetery. Pollution to kill 'em, religion to save 'em, and oak trees to bury 'em under, Dix always thought. The houses on the single lane side-streets are a mishmash of weathered wooden Cracker houses, peeling Victorians, and red brick ranches. The only sidewalk runs the length of Main Street, docks to mill, and the only stop sign is where Main Street dead-ends at

7

the river. Dix always loved the view from that stop sign.

She stood there this early Wednesday, and she remembered the summers when she was a kid, when she had come back to the Point to get away . . . got sent away is more like it, she thought. The STOP was an upside-down exclamation point between her and the river. Only one shrimp boat still rocked at the dock, and the dawn sky was pink through the dark lines of shrimp net stretched between mast and deck. Dix yawned, hands in pockets, and blinked back the mist of morning or too little sleep. Buddy had worked for Dad during summer vacations back then, Mom taught summer school, Dix got sent back to the Point . . . away from them . . . exile. And now I'm back again . . . self-exile, she supposed.

Dix knew she was putting off going back to the house. Iris was there. Hurting. Dying. She let her eyes follow a gull as it skimmed the surface of the brown river. This time she had come back to help her mom take care of Iris. The unmarried daughter's duty, Dix thought, and couldn't help but smile.

That's what her lover, Sarah, had said when Dix told her she was going back to the Point for the summer to take care of a dying grandmother. "The unmarried daughter's duty," Sarah had laughed.

The white bird faded into the haze and Dix blinked. She bit her lip. That had been before she had told Sarah that she also wanted to think about breaking up.

Dix pressed her fingers into her temples, blinked and rolled her neck to crack it. Everything ends, she thought. The stop sign darkened as the sky behind it lightened. It was something Iris had said: "Ever'thang

8

ends." Iris, Dix thought, Iris, who is the Point. Iris, who had chosen to die.

Iris had always done whatever she damned well pleased. When Dix had come back every summer, Iris had let her do as she pleased too. Dix knew that was part of why she loved her grandmother so much . . . why they loved each other so much. Iris had let her be whatever she wanted; she had let her just be a kid. I suppose she's doing what she damned well pleases now, Dix thought, choosing to die. Choosing to die. Dix wondered, will I cease to be a kid?

"You were never a kid," Sarah had said. "Until you met me." It was true. Dix knew it was true. Even though she had been free those summers with Iris, it'd been too late for Dix to really be a kid. She'd already gotten serious. Sarah though, Sarah had let her play . . . made her play.

Dix remembered the long, tanned arm reaching toward her from a wide oak limb, coaxing, and the red-brown tangle of curls lifting in the breeze. That day Sarah's eyes had been the same blue as the sky beyond. *She does bring out that kid in me.* Dix blinked and the net of the shrimp boat focused. "Come on, you're never too old to climb trees!" Sarah had called, and up Dix had gone . . . thirty years old, climbing trees, nestling into the crook of a branch, Sarah's arms around her. She makes me play, Dix thought, lets me play, inspires me to play. "I'll always let you be a kid," Sarah had said. "But I do want a commitment. I can't let you be a kid about that." Dix sighed and rubbed the warmth back into her arms. I can't help it, she thought, and shook her head. Damn, I miss her.

I sure didn't miss John when I came back to the

Point after our divorce, she thought, studying the pattern of webbing against pale blue sky; I didn't miss him any of those times I came back when I left him. Dix crossed her arms. The morning breeze curled inland, chilly, off the river. She wondered again, so why did I go back to John over and over?

She let her mind follow the familiar path of questions, her eyes stopping at a ragged hole in the shrimp net draped against dawn. I knew it wasn't working; I knew it was stupid; I knew he wasn't what I wanted; I knew a *he* wasn't what I wanted... Okay, so why? Why eight years? Shit. If Sarah were here, she'd cut me right off, Dix thought, and allowed herself a little smile. "No regrets," Sarah would say. No Sarah, Dix thought. Streaks of pink-fringed thin white clouds toward the east. Eight years married. Eight years of working on something that would never work. Why? Shit, she thought, why does Mom stay with Dad? Why does Buddy stay with Dad? Why doesn't Iris go for the chemo? Why do I keep coming back to Point Will, Georgia? No answers. Dix allowed herself a little smile. "No regrets," she murmured.

Dix put her palm flat on the cool red of the stop sign. Back to the Point again. This stop sign had seen her grow up. She had come here from Jacksonville, summer after summer, to try to be a kid. She had stood here, hand cool against STOP, thinking of her father and God and her mother and her brother and her books and her grandmother and boys and girls and the Point. She had come here when she dropped out of college. She had come here after that day her Dad had found her with John, had seen that they were "living in sin," and had stood on the hot driveway in front of the trailer and yelled, "Whore!" for the whole neighborhood to hear. Dix had stood here with her hand flat and cool on the sign that day. They didn't speak for two years after that.

And then I went away, she thought, but I still came back to the Point when I needed to try to figure things out ... The half dozen times I left John, after I divorced him, when I made love to that first woman, when that first woman dumped me, after Mom cried when I told her I was gay, when Mom said she still loved me and Dad said not a word.

And he hasn't said a word since.

Oh, well. And now I'm back here again.

She looked out to the place where the river and the sea and the sky blurred together in gray. Getting nowhere. No answers. Sarah in St. Pete whispered "No regrets" at the back of Dix's mind, and she smiled, then felt the corners of her mouth slacken, remembering. No Sarah. Or maybe Sarah. Or maybe not. She frowned.

Dix stretched and rubbed dew from her arms. She reviewed the situation. She had quit her teaching job without tenure ... not that they'd give it to a dyke anyway. She needed to choose between grad school in Florida, home, or two thousand miles north in New York, and she had no idea how she was going to pay for it. With Sarah or without Sarah. I'm spending my summer with my mother, who will likely make me as crazy as she is, Dix thought, and my father is a thundering silence. And Iris is dying. Back to the Point, but where?

The decimal point is a place of absolute zero, absolute nothingness. In one direction is the positive; in the other direction is the negative. By remaining at the point, or beginning at the point, or returning to the point, I come back to nothingness.

I'm no mathematician, or much of a philosopher, for that matter, but now that I'm back for the first time since that summer when Grandma died, I begin to understand the importance of that landmark ... zero.

Here, at the little desk in the downstairs bedroom,

as I write that summer down, I move away and back all in one motion. I fall into that summer, the last summer the Point really lived for me, the last summer Iris lived; I fall inside the screen of the computer, inside my self, and lose the Point where I exist. The now. And then the mailman rattles the box on the front porch, or a visitor crunches the gravel of the front drive, and I return to this Point. Will the visitor or the letter-writer be Sarah? Mom? Dad? Bud? Some ghost of the Point?

It is a huge 0, a circle, a zero. The Point.

Catch of the Day

When she looked in on Iris before leaving for her walk, Dix saw her grandmother's hands gripping the blankets and the lines deep in her forehead, and she knew it was going to be a bad day. Her mother had opened her eyes from the cot beside Iris's bed and shook her head silently, motioning Dix away. It was over an hour yet until the next pain meds, no need to chance waking her. Dix and Betty had fallen into a comfortable routine, alternating nights of sleeping on the cot, napping during the afternoon to catch up.

On the bad days, Dix agreed with her mother that sleep was a blessing for them all.

"Catching up" was actually how they spent all of the good days, Dix mused. The breeze from the ocean, the sun huge and orange beyond the dark trees of the Island, bent the marsh grass and the hairs on her arms inland. Past the stop sign and the docks she recognized the faint blush of the clay cliff on the Florida side, the river a good two or three miles wide here at its mouth, winding brown and thick between mud flats and green marsh. Just yesterday she had sat there on the dock with Iris, listening again to the story of Roses Bluff.

"I knew it'd be a rain before the day was out," Iris said, "but I just had a hankerin' for a picnic. The kids was about to drive me batty with bein' bored from bein' outa school 'n I knew them blackberries 'd be fat over there. Me 'n Cap both always loved a blackberry cobbler in the summertime. He was already out shrimpin' by the time I got the notion to take the young'uns over to the Bluff, of course. Still early, though. Nobody much stayed abed till after six in them days . . . less 'n they were drinkers 'n such.

"Sos anyway, I got the kids together 'n all packed up, 'n we set out on the turn of the tide. The only way you could go, of course, was to ride the tide goin' in over to the Bluff and the tide goin' out back to the Point. My biggest boy, your Uncle Don, was a good big fella by then, maybe thirteen, 'n he helped me out with the rowin' pretty good. Your daddy was all the time wantin' to help, but he was mostly a nuisance, you know how that age is, splashin' the girls 'n squirmin' about. He never did sit still good. Seems like I was always sayin', 'Ed stop that 'n sit still.' Anyways, we got over to Roses Bluff near about eleven as I recollect. Hot day, too. And I just set 'em loose. Ate our sandwiches 'n told 'em to each bring back one bowl of berries 'n not get in no trouble. Shoulda knowed Ed'd be the one."

Dix loved this part of the story. She couldn't imagine her Dad, man of a million rules, as the hellion Iris made him out to be. She twisted, pulling one foot up onto the bench, so she could watch Iris's face. Was she tired? Should she stop her and take her home?

The clear eyes were focused far across the river. Iris smiled. "Reckon I shouldn't 'a let 'em take off like that. Honest truth was, I just wanted 'em gone for awhile. I leaned up against one of them dead trees that had fallen off the top of the bluff, and I went plumb to sleep. Nothin' like a nap after dinner. Anyways, next thing I know there's all this screamin' and a-yellin' like I don't know what all. Seems like that Ed'd gone 'n got hisself sprayed by a skunk. Lord-a-mighty, what a racket he did raise. Hooo-ee, what a smell. The other kids were laughin' and backin' away from him, and he was a-cryin' and spittin' and dancin' outa his clothes just as fast as he could. I just didn't know what to do, between scoldin' him and scoldin' the others 'n tryin' to keep outa smellin' range myself."

Iris paused and her grin faded to serious. Dix felt

her own face straighten. Iris focused in on a shabby gull standing on one foot near the water.

"I reckon I shouldn't 'a left him there, all by hisself. Only ten, I reckon, but the other young'uns absolutely refused to get into that rowboat with him. I couldn't leave Don with 'em 'cuz I needed him to help row, and the girls was just too young. Cap should've been able to get over and get back well before dark, but that danged storm kicked up fast."

Dix followed Iris's clear gray gaze across the width of brown river to the pinkish Florida cliff. She imagined how far away the Point must have looked to a lonely, smelly ten-year-old (younger even than her own students). He would have been able to see the stacks of the mill, and the docks and maybe the steeple of the Episcopal church above the trees. He would be able to watch the progress of the rowboat until the rain started, and then he would have to wait in the darkness for the low chug of the shrimp boat under the whine of wind. Dix wondered if he cried. She didn't think so.

"That poor child was the pitifulest sight I ever did see. Cap 'n me had to scold the others to keep 'em from laughin', but it was a might hard to hold it in ourselves. We scrubbed him up good, but he stunk for a good two weeks anyway. I remember eating blackberry cobbler out there on the front porch with him all alone 'cuz he was too embarrassed to come inside. Even slept out there for awhile. Poor child. Never did go over to Roses Bluff again."

Iris sighed at the end of a long silence. "Take me home, child. I'm plumb tuckered."

The skin of the arm Dix supported was as thin

and dry as October corn husks, and Iris shook her head even as she collapsed into the front seat of Dix's car. "Have to *ride* three blocks to sit in the sun and do nothin' and I *still* get wore out. Reckon these docks won't be seein' much 'a me no more, much less the ol' Bluff." Her thin fingers had grasped the dashboard as she pulled herself forward for a long look.

Dix sat still. Iris shook her head sharply and thopped Dix's arm. "Well, what are you waitin' for? Get that air goin' girl, it's hot enough in here to burst a dead cat."

Dix leaned her forehead against the cool metal STOP, and looked down at gray sand pitted with ant lion dens. Maybe her dad was an abused child. That's surely what the counselors at the school would say. Betty had said it many times. And Mom should know, Dix thought, she sees the same kids in elementary school who become my screwed up teenagers. Really just another excuse for him, though. Her fingers climbed the ladder of holes up the sign post. Of course, her mother made as many excuses for Iris as she did for Ed. "Doin' the best she knew how; all of us doin' the best we know how."

Dix pushed herself back and away from her sign, patting it on each side of the STOP with both palms. The sun had just cleared the treetops on the Island. "Best," she murmured to herself, turning to face Main Street into town. "Some excuse."

18

*T*he Point is one long story for me. Iris's long tales of the people, the family, the place weave in and around themselves, like the soap opera she watched every day at two o'clock. "My story," she called it. "Can't miss my story," she'd say, and take up her needle and thread and settle in front of the big TV for an hour. The Point was my soap opera, my story, and I'd settle on the cool cement of the front porch in the late afternoon, and Iris would relate another episode which I'd catalog away to try and make sense of later.

Most of what I do these days is try to make sense of Iris's stories. I wrote a story about the family of a shrimper and a storm and Roses Bluff... "Catch of the Day." It won me a fellowship. I shaped my story to make a meaning, to have a point. Did Iris's stories have a point?

In this now, five years later, I write about Iris's last summer, my last summer at the Point, and I want to know did that summer, that weekend, have a point? How can I find my way to that Point?

Bird Songs and Circles

"No excuse for you to behave in such a way, Ed."
Dix heard her mother's voice in the front hallway,
hushed, but echoing up the front stairway and back
down the kitchen stairs. Dix closed the screen door
softly and stood rubbing her arms in the entry, still
chilled with the wind off the marsh. "She's still your
daughter, Ed." Betty's whisper drifted down in dust
motes. "She *is* still your daughter." Dix looked
around at the raincoats and fishing hats on hooks
then back up the stairs, waiting. "Well, she's still *my*
daughter, and I love her even if she *is* one of *them*."

Dix smiled down at the worn steps. "You can at least be polite to her, Ed. For your poor mother's sake if for nothing else."

The tarnished doorknob into the kitchen was cool and wobbly under Dix's hand. She could smell the coffee she'd put on before she went out for her walk, but she hesitated another minute. She smiled at herself, eavesdropping on her mother's phone call. Her grandmother had always called her the "listenin' child." "You're the one they had in mind when they made up that sayin' 'bout little pitchers with big ears," Iris used to say and wink. "Good for you," she'd whisper.

Betty's voice rose to a normal tone. "Well, we'll be looking for you about noon then. You bring Buddy along too now, you hear?"

Dix smiled and reopened the screen door and let it slam shut. If she had to endure dinner with Dad, at least her brother, Buddy, would be there to take some of the flak. Good old Bud, why on earth would anyone keep working for a father like Ed? Dix shook her head, still smiling as she turned the wobbly knob into the kitchen. Betty's "Bye, bye now" bounced in through the dining room, and Dix poured two cups of coffee.

"Mornin', Mom." Her mother's grin always amazed Dix, perfectly unconscious, teeth bowed out and crooked, and completely beautiful. Like a child's, she thought.

"Good morning, daughter." Betty hugged Dix with one arm and took the proffered coffee cup in the other hand. "Beautiful morning, isn't it? Oh, look at the cardinal!" She stood for a second, both hands cupped around the warm mug, gazing out the tall window at the bird feeder. "I just think they're the most beautiful birds," she murmured.

Dix looked at the shadow of her mother's body against the window through the thin nylon nightgown and realized that her mother seemed smaller. She stooped a little in the morning chill, and her breasts sagged. Dix smiled at the outline of her mother's waist-high panties . . . she and Sarah had been laughing, *playing,* in the lingerie department at Sears in St. Pete just last week. "Will you still love me when I wear bloomers like these?" she had asked. "Like our mothers wear?" Dix grinned just as her mother turned and smiled back, just like a child.

Will I indeed, Dix wondered, studying the soft sag of her mother's form, her beautiful, playful smile.

"Look at you, grinnin' like a Cheshire cat." Betty tilted her head. "What's got you so all-fired smiley this mornin'?"

Dix paused. "Actually, I was thinking of Sarah," she said.

Betty's smile vanished and small creases appeared across her brow. "Oh." She looked away from Dix's eyes and down at her coffee cup. "Um," she stopped. "Um, how is Sarah?"

"Good." It was Dix's turn to stop and examine her coffee. "Good, fine, um . . ." She looked up and quickly past her mother to where the cardinal had been joined by his mate. The male flung seeds from the feeder in a busy spray. "Sarah's good," she said softly, staring out the window. She glanced at her mother's eyes. "She wants to go up north with me in the fall if I go there."

Betty looked down. "Oh."

The clock in the front hallway cuckooed seven.

Betty walked to the coffee pot, and Dix turned and moved closer to the window, the two women circling apart. Glass clinked against cup. The birds started up and cocked their heads around. The dusky female fluttered to regain her perch. Dix felt Betty watching her back.

"I don't know if I want her to come with me," she said to the glass. "You know. I, I think maybe it's a bad idea for someone to change their life for another person." Her fingertip rubbed warm circles on her cup. "What if it doesn't work out? You're stuck." Her voice became steadily softer. "It's harder to get out if you've changed things . . . moved somewhere . . . What if you're not ready? What if it's not right? You're stuck." Dix's voice trailed away and the kitchen was silent for a long moment. She thought of her marriage to John, again. "I'm not sure. I don't know," she finally said, turning abruptly for the coffee pot. The cardinals flashed away red, startled.

"I liked Sarah," Betty said.

Dix remembered the meeting in St. Pete, her mother and her lover laughing over pasta at Anna's, the other customers smiling their way. "Are *all* these people, uh, you know?" Betty had whispered across the table, glancing around. "They look so normal." Sarah had winked and nodded, slyly. "All except the mothers," she had whispered back.

Dix smiled. "Yeah," she said softly, "I like Sarah, too." The phrase echoed for a second. Like her, love her, leave her, Dix thought. How?

Betty picked up a dishrag from the sink and began to wipe the counters. "Well, I just can't tell you what to do. Just put it in the Lord's hands, and, well, of course . . ." She concentrated on the counters and the dishrag under her palm, rubbing furiously. "Well, Sarah is a nice girl, Dixie." Betty nodded to herself, frowning. "But, well, of course, you know..." She gave her head a quick shake. "I've just put it in the Lord's hands."

Smiling to herself, Dix took a sip of her coffee and leaned back on the mantel. Thanks Mom, she thought.

"Lord's hands," Betty murmured, dusting on into the dining room.

Iris swirled in a place where pain was a tide pulling her away from a safe dream. Dix watched her grandmother's eyelids twitch and the throb of pulse at her temple. At least now when she woke up it would be time for the next dose of pain meds. Today will be a bad one, she thought. Hold onto that wave, Iris.

Since Dix had arrived, Iris had had only one really bad day. Mostly it had been easy to imagine that this was just another in the chain of summers in Point Will, long days of iced tea in sweaty glasses and Iris's stories in the shade of the pecan tree.

Except that I'm older, Dix thought. Except that Iris's voice weakens before the end of the story, except that Mom is here. Exceptions to all the old rules. Rules. Dear old Dad. Not here, here, silent, and exception. Sarah. Exceptions to rules.

Iris licked her lips, eyes still closed, and gripped the blankets. Dix sat down on the bed beside her and the eyelids fluttered open. Iris grinned weakly.

"Good morning, Grandma." Dix propped her up

with one arm and held a glass to her lips to chase the pills down.

Iris leaned back on the pillows and closed her eyes for a minute. "Oh, I wish I didn't need to get up to use the pot," she groaned. She opened her eyes as Dix opened her mouth. "Don't you even think about tryin' t' get me on that bedpan, neither, missy." Iris smiled to soften it and murmured, "Just let me get woke up good first. I ain't 'bout so dead yet I can't get up to pee." She stared at the ceiling.

"Mornin' sleepyhead." Betty followed her dust rag in. "How are you feelin' this fine mornin', Mother?" She bent over Iris and smoothed the white waves of hair back from her forehead gently.

"Just grand." Iris closed her eyes on her daughter-in-law's face.

"Have you been to the potty yet, Mother?" Betty bent and reached under the bed and the metal pan clanged against something. "I don't think it's a good idea for you to be getting up just —"

"I will pee when I want to and where I want to and I am not one of your first-grade children." Voice deepening as she spoke, each word distinct, Iris pulled herself up and away from the pillows into Betty's face.

"But . . ."

"Go dust now," Iris said, "dear."

Betty turned and mouthed "I'll check back" to Dix on her way out.

Iris held herself stiff until the door pulled softly shut behind Betty, then crumpled back. "Humph."

Dix shook her head while Iris caught her breath. "Why the hell does she just take it from you like that, Grandma?"

Iris opened her eyes slowly. "She takes it 'cuz she likes it, child. You know that." She closed her eyes again. "You heard 'a Joan of Arc. Same thing. Glory." Iris sighed. "The real question, child, is if we don't like the martyr thing, why do we keep lettin' her do it?" She grabbed Dix's hand sharply. Her fingers were still strong; they bit into Dix's wrist. "What grief you give her, child?"

Dix was quiet. Iris always asked the hard questions. Finally she said, "I think you're wrong, Grandma. I try to be nice to Mom." Not like you and Dad, she thought.

The hold on her hand was tight and dry. How could a dying woman be so strong? "Oh, but you give her grief, child, you know you do." Iris's grip suddenly loosened and she patted the back of Dix's hand. "It's okay, though, you're doin' the best you can."

The room became very still. They could both hear Betty humming as she worked. "Occurs to me," Iris began softly. "Occurs to me, you were quite a bit like your mother, that Joan 'a Arc thing, when you was married to that fella John. Reckon you oughta understand it purty clear, child."

Dix smiled. "At least I didn't let 'em burn me at the stake, huh Grandma?" Though I know that's just what Dad has in mind for me these days, she continued to herself. Out of the fire . . . She smiled.

" 'Potty,' " Iris snorted toward the ceiling. "Never even said that to my children. 'Go potty.' Humph." She smiled weakly at Dix. "Reckon I'd better think about doin' it though . . . lessin' you wanta have to change these here sheets."

Iris reached out her arms toward Dix, who pulled

her upright in a hug. Iris rested her full weight on
Dix's shoulder for a long moment. It was the weight
of a thin adolescent. Iris breathed hard. Dix rubbed
the nylon-sheathed bones of her grandmother's back
slowly. Iris breathed in heavily and inched a leg
toward the bedside.

"You don't have to do this, you know," Dix said
softly.

Iris stopped moving and sighed. She rested her
head again on her granddaughter's shoulder. "I
know."

They listened in silence to Betty greeting the
mailman on the front porch, neither moving, Betty's
voice musical and her tone too happy. Iris sighed
again. "Just, these little battles seem so damned
important now. Seem like I give in to the bedpan,
I'm losin' somethin' important." She shook her head
back and forth against Dix's shoulder, then leaned
back into her pillows. "Just pride, I reckon."

Dix smiled and Iris took her hand. "Actually, I
think them pills is startin' to work a bit," she said.
"I do feel a little better."

She inched her legs toward the edge of the bed
and Dix helped her swing them over. She put her
arm around Iris's waist and they sat for a second
while she caught her breath. "Okay child," Iris said
finally, "let's go potty."

Dix sat on the foot of Iris's bed, legs crossed, the
letter from Sarah smooth in her hands. Betty brushed
her mother-in-law's hair in slow steady strokes, both

women so silent Dix could hear the crackle of static electricity. She concentrated on an edited reading of the letter.

" 'Dear Dix,' " she read aloud, "Um... 'I hope your grandmother is doing well. I know how important it is to you to be with her now...' " Dix's eyes skimmed ahead across the familiar tall slanting script. "She's working hard. There're some pictures from the newspaper here that she did, front page of the fashion section. 'The model was a b —' She didn't like the model. Blah, blah, blah... 'some mail for you from N.Y.U. and the University of Florida.' " Dix looked up for a second. "Maybe about the grants." She smiled at her mother and grandmother, Iris's eyes closed, Betty's hands draped with her silver- white hair. Betty sighed. Dix continued, "Um, 'anyway, after I finish shooting those portfolios for Michelle, I'm done for a while. So I'm coming to the P —' Shi —" Dix's voice dropped and her eyes raced across the paper. "She's coming to the Point."

She looked up and met her mother's eyes. Betty was frozen in mid-brush-stroke. Dix said, "She'll be here Friday."

Iris opened her eyes and grinned. "Well, fine, fine, ain't that fine? I been wantin' to meet this here Sarah. Of course she's welcome to stay a spell."

Dix forced her eyes to focus on her grandmother. "Are you sure? I can call and tell her you're not up to it if you want." Dix heard a note of hope in her voice. Did *she* want Sarah at the Point?

Iris shrugged. "Shoo girl, any young folks is better 'n these old buzzards who keep circlin' by to see if I've kicked off yet." She looked at Dix sharply.

"This house is plenty big enough for one more. You know that. The day I'm not up to comp'ny is the day you can plant me in the ground."

Betty had been sitting quietly, looking worried. "She is a nice girl, Dixie," she said slowly. "I'm sure she won't be a bit of a bother." She stopped and cleared her throat with a short cough. "She can sleep in the front east bedroom."

Iris looked at Betty, frowning. "What's wrong with the other single in Dixie's room? Don't tell me the boards've gone and fallen again. Cap never did replace them danged things. I pestered him up to the day he died to get to that . . ." Her voice trailed off. "It's too danged hot ta sleep late in that front room."

Betty was staring hard at her daughter. "Of course Sarah will sleep in the front east room. She'll be happier there, I'm sure."

Dix smiled and shook her head. "Sure, Mom, whatever."

Iris looked from one to the other and shook her head. "Thought you stopped hearin' *other* people when you got old, not the other way 'round." She leaned forward between the two. "*What's wrong with the bed in Dix's room?*"

Dix smiled and took her hand. "Nothing, Grandma. It's fine."

Betty jumped in. "I'm just sure Sarah will be more comfortable in the front east bedroom . . . all that light . . . and you said yourself, we have enough empty rooms for an army here."

Iris shook her head. Looking into Dix's eyes, she squeezed her hand. "Well, your friend is welcome anywhere in my house she wants to stay."

Behind her grandmother, Dix could see Betty scowling at her and shaking her head firmly, no. Dix grinned and pulled Iris into a hug. "Thank you, Grandma."

*O*n a map, in two dimensions, the way to the Point is straightforward. Just follow the road from the Interstate until it dead-ends. And it is easy . . . if all you want is to get there.

You do have to choose to go there, as Grandma always pointed out. Its not on the way to anyplace else, it's at the end of the road. If you make a wrong turn, you find water . . . the wide river, the ocean, then marsh . . . In storms, the road is often swallowed by the sea at high tide; the Point can become an island.

The road is usually a scenic route, and it's easy to

be distracted. I often pull over at one of the dozen or so bridges to inhale the salt and listen to the tide rustling the marsh grass. My eyes will wander off into the trees or sky beyond the river, and I will be startled by the thunder of a passing log truck a long time later, as if I have dozed. There are places where the arms of oak trees have been amputated at the edge of the road, and still they reach higher across and dangle gray moss in shadows. Sometimes a clump will drop with a soft thump on the windshield as I drive, and I'll realize that the car has been following the road without my conscious control. Some circuit pathway is worn with many tracks into my brain. I find my way to the Point as if in a dream.

Southern Belles
and Whistles

Iris slept on her back, emitting a faint snore with every rise of the white sheets. She seemed to be pain-free, eyelids twitching in dream. Dix folded the letter from Sarah and rubbed the sharp paper edge against her lip.

The room seemed to have never changed. It was the only downstairs bedroom, the one where people came to die.

Dix remembered her great-grandmother in this same bed, and her grandpa, Cap, before that. Dix remembered playing hide 'n seek behind the filmy white curtains, scaring her little brother, Buddy, when she appeared, moaning that she was the angel of death. It was a cool, dark room, shaded on the east by the cedars lining the drive, and on the north by the two stories of front porches. It had been empty for most of her childhood, except when the house was filled with out-of-town relatives on holidays or when someone got ready to die.

It was a good room to be sick in, Dix knew. Putting the letter into her book she prowled the perimeter, tracing the dust on the mantel, petting the soft leaves of the African violets in the window. Great-great grandmother grimaced in fading brown, her portrait over the fireplace commanding the entire room. A baseball bat leaned against the crooks of umbrellas in their stand. Dix drew it out, slid her palm down the smooth length of wood, weighed it. Ed's bat. "Bet I can still hit homers with it," he'd always said. She wrinkled her nose at a whiff of the dinner Betty was cooking, mustard greens, ugh. Ed's favorite. He'd be here soon, grumbling if they weren't sitting down when the noon whistle blew.

She had wakened in this room once on a muggy Fourth of July afternoon, her head exploding. She remembered opening her left eye, something cold and clammy draped over the right. At first she thought it was there to hold her brains in; they felt like they were trying to gush out, pushing and pounding against the eye socket. She had been able to see enough through her left — dust motes and the huge oval portrait of the grim woman — to know she was in the downstairs bedroom. That had been enough to convince her she was about to die.

"Lord, Ed," she'd heard Iris whisper, "you whapped her a good one when you slung that bat. She's gonna have a shiner for sure. Lucky you didn't do worse."

"Lucky school's out," Dix's mother had muttered to the sheet she was smoothing. "Child ab —"

"Aw Mama." Ed's voice had sounded odd, boyish. "It was just a accident, you know that." He paused and Dix had opened her eye again. "Hit a good long homer, though, didn't I?" He thwapped the bat against his palm, then stroked the smooth length of wood. He noticed Dix squinting at him. "Can't expect a girl to know not to play catcher so close without a mask, eh, Sissy?"

The pounding behind the steak on Dix's eye intensified. She closed her eye and thought she could see the blood.

"Buddy'll show you the right way sometime," Ed continued in darkness. "Ask 'im."

Dix watched Iris sleeping. It should have been Buddy anyway, she thought. He had always been the one in the way of Ed's "accidents." Buddy had never mastered adolescent invisibility like Dix had, and he had the scars to prove it. Yep, she had learned one thing from her brother, how to stay out of the way . . . except that one time.

She had spent two days in this room wearing steak on her eye. "Waste of perfectly good meat," the doctor had snorted, but Ed had insisted. "Got t' have raw meat on a black eye," he had said, "and only the best for my little girl. Two dollars a pound."

Dix had felt uneasy. They explained she had to sleep in this room because they were worried she'd get dizzy on the stairs. She didn't sleep much during those two days. Not only did her brains hurt, not only did Ed drop in every day, this was the room people died in.

Iris snored on. The best thing about this room was that you knew everything that went on downstairs. It opened onto the living room at the back of the house, and the long drive passed just outside the tall windows. Whether company parked in the back by the garage and gardenia bushes or on the street under the oaks, the occupant of this room knew of visitors first. The convenience of the ground floor and the adjoining bathroom might have been the main reason the old and the sick were housed here, but the echoing of voices in the front hallway, even drifting from upstairs, through the bathroom, the TV chatter from the living room, the slow, hushed laughter and squeak-rock of chairs on the front porch, and the crunch of cars on the shell drive, seemed now to Dix a covert ploy to keep the dying pulled back into life. And it worked. Cap had held on months longer than the doctors predicted. Dix herself had crept out to the kitchen for midnight snacks, shiner thudding her forehead. She grinned, remembering the moon on the kitchen floor, and the steak left on the kitchen table, blood puddled and sticky by morning. "Reckon you're gonna live," Iris had said, and Dix's stay in the downstairs room had ended.

The drive crunched with the weight of Ed's pickup truck. Dix saw its orange-yellow home paint job bounce past through the thin white curtains. Dix hugged herself, wrapping her arms around, feeling her ribs draw in, then shook her head sharply as she recognized the motion. No. Stiff and slow, she stretched her arms back and over her head, squared her shoulders and breathed in, inhaling hints of dinner: corn bread, fried fish, mustards. The back screen door into the living room slammed, and she flinched.

Iris stirred, one leg flexing then relaxing quickly. Her breath evened again, and Dix stood and grabbed the edge of the mantel and twisted her torso, her back cracking. She was getting nowhere in her book. She shrugged to the portrait over the fireplace; one of her mother's romances, the book had probably been written before even great-great grandma's time. Maybe a trip to the library this afternoon. She tried not to listen for her dad.

The TV came on in the next room ... He was checking *Headline News,* or was it the Weather Channel? At least the volume was low. Iris didn't move. Betty's murmur. Dix looked up and into great-great's eyes, bent closer. The woman frowned into the distance, away from the camera, into a high corner of the room. This fireplace backed the living room fireplace, chimneys connected above, and Betty's whisper floated down like smoke into the room. It became more animated.

". . . your mother . . . room . . . just can't explain . . ." Dix smiled at her brown-on-brown tinted ancestor. Great-great seemed to frown more furiously. Ed's voice, suddenly loud. "Won't have it. Sodom 'n Gomorrah under my own mama's roof. You just tell her she can't have that ... *person* ... here."

Iris groaned, and Dix looked quickly over to her. She seemed to be still asleep.

"Shhh ... your mother." Betty's whisper became urgent. "... *is* your mother's house ... already invited the woman."

Dix rolled her eyes to the ceiling. "The woman." Sarah would get a kick out of that.

Betty's voice dwindled. Ed's grumbled. Dix watched Iris lying very still, and wondered. Betty's tone became matter-of-fact. "... must protect your mother ... simply cannot know about Dixie ... her condition ..." Ed's grunt was incoherent. "I'll speak to her ... don't upset ..." Dix heard her father's low grumble interrupt Betty. "Please be nice to her, Ed ... for your mother's sake." The voices faded into the kitchen and a rattle of pots and pans.

Dix turned back to the huge oval portrait over the fireplace. "For your mother's sake," she murmured to the dusty woman in the picture. "Humph." For her own part, she wasn't so sure Iris hadn't figured things out. Mostly, Dix figured Iris wouldn't much give a damn anyway. She had been all set to tell her grandmother she was a lesbian when she told everybody else two years ago, but Cap'd just died, and it seemed like more had been said in those few days than ever before. Ed had finally imposed his silence, and Betty had worn out her tear ducts and Dix remembered feeling she had simply exhausted all the words. She had let Betty convince her to keep Iris innocent, "at least."

Dix shook her head slowly. *For your mother's sake.* A truck door slammed out front — Buddy — and Iris stretched, opened her gray eyes and smiled.

"I reckon I do feel a mite better," she said, and pulled herself up to lean against the headboard. Dix reached behind her and plumped the pillows. At the sound of the noon whistle from the mill, Iris shook her head. "I declare, this has been one long morning, hasn't it, child? Over the hump of the week now, though."

"Sleepin' your life away, Mama." Ed stuck his head in the door, then realized what he'd said. "Uh." He swallowed. Dix felt herself begin to smile and squelched it, watching her dad. He didn't allow himself to look at her. "Uh, Betty says do you want your dinner on a tray or do you feel up to eatin' at the table?"

Iris didn't answer.

"Oh, she'll be up all right." Buddy came in through the bathroom, huge and grinning. "Even if I have t' carry her in."

"You get that pipe loaded?" Ed put his body in the doorway, his tone that of a boss. "Got to get that job finished tonight, don't care how late."

Buddy shrugged. "Yes sir, we're all set." He stood, arms crossed and feet planted. Ed humphed and backed out, Iris's glare following him. "Hey, Grandma." Buddy sat down on the bed, dwarfing Iris, and wrapped one arm around her. "Hey, Sis." He grinned at Dix.

"Buddy-boy." Dix watched as her hulk of a little brother pulled Iris into a hug. His smile was a mirror of their mother's, slightly bucktoothed, a little snaggled, and beautiful over his grandmother's shoulder. How does he do that, Dix wondered. Big and gentle, a sort of La-Z-Boy lounger of a human, Bud hugged people naturally, easily. Dix was still usually a self-conscious hugger; she had had to learn it like a skill. She was a little jealous of the way Bud walked into hugs like breathing. How did he ever learn that? He winked at her.

"Where are those great-grandbabies of mine?" Iris demanded, pushing Bud away.

Bud stood up and smoothed the sheet, answering, "Melissa's on her way, Grandma. They'll be here."

"She's late," Iris said. "Always eat at noon. Oughta be sayin' the blessin' right now." She began to slide her legs over the side of the bed and scoot forward. "That girl's always late."

*I*t's been five years since that last time I came to the Point. Time is important.

The Point no longer exists outside of time. The Navy has built a base for nuclear submarines just beyond the city limits, just beyond the mill, and the road into town is now littered with bars and uniforms and fast food emporiums. Still, one does have to slow down as one nears the end of the road, the STOP sign, and the Point is just a beat behind the rest of the world.

I can depend on time here. The noon whistle

blows, the cemetery fills front to back, chronologically, the Washington oak is a sprout again, genetically engineered from the original root. My family is born, ages, dies, and is reborn. The stories flash back and forward. I am always in the now. Each instant, each point is a new point of departure. And the same Point has always been.

High Noon

Iris fidgeted at the head of the long table. Ed stood at the other end, solemn all the way from his shock of glued-in-place gray hair to his clasped hands and his wingtips. Betty brought in the last of the steaming bowls. Iris glared at the four empty chairs, two stacked with phone books. "We'll start without 'em."

"Father in heaven," Ed began, and Dix glanced up at the slam of car doors on the street. Ed's voice deepened and kept its cadence. "We come to you today . . ." A child's voice screamed, "He hit me!"

"Begging forgiveness..." Ed intoned. Small feet clattered on the front porch, just through the dining room window. "He hit me first," another one called from the street. "...FOR OUR MANY SINS," Ed boomed.

Dix looked over at him. Yeah right, Dad.

A baby began to shriek outside. Ed continued his prayer as the doorbell began ringing and ringing and ringing. Buddy had his head studiously bowed, eyes closed. Dix wished he'd look up so they could grin at each other; no kid could resist that old-fashioned doorbell. "Shush, shhh," she heard Melissa in the front hallway. Dix saw her mother across the table frown at the open door behind Dix and bring her finger to her lips, then close her eyes again.

"... blessing on this food, oh Lord," Ed continued, "and on this family here today."

" 'Men!" shouted a voice from the door, followed by a small stampede. "Grandpa, Grandpa!"

Ed gave up and reached down for one boy wrapped around his legs, roughly mussing the hair of the other. Dix grinned her hello to Melissa who was handing the baby off to an already babbling Betty.

"Late, Missy," Iris said, helping herself to a steaming mound of white rice.

Melissa shrugged and sat down. "It's not easy gettin' this crew anywhere on time." She began dishing food onto plates. "You boys get settled down and let your grandpa eat."

Melissa was young and beautiful and brilliant, but it was all buried inside about ten extra pounds per kid. Dix had watched this girth grow with each pregnancy, slowly suffocating the girl who had won a half scholarship five years before. "Red won't eat sweet potatoes, Mama," she said and busily scraped them onto her own plate. She half-smiled and shrugged her shoulder at Dix across the table, not meeting her eyes, "Eatin' for two . . ."

Dix saw Ed scowl, watching him from the corner of her eye, an old habit, and she unconsciously straightened her spine and drew her elbows into her body. "Already got enough for all the children in Ethiopia, I'd say," he muttered.

The little boys on either side of him became quiet immediately, the older one slipping his hands into his lap and sitting up straight.

Melissa put down her fork deliberately, pushed her chair back from the table, slung the diaper bag over one shoulder, and reached down for the baby. "Let's go to Burger King, guys."

Betty blustered, the baby spoon halfway in, "Oh, what's the matter? Where are you taking . . . Ed?" The baby's open mouth followed the swerving spoon.

Dix watched her father. He looked up from his plate, surprised. "Hmm? Huh?" He looked from one grandson to the other. "You boys aren't leavin' your old grandad, are you?" He wore his innocent face. "Finish everything on those plates before you leave the table, eh?" He leaned to Red, between him and Dix. "Pass me the peas, will ya, boy?"

Red, already used to the routine at five, leaned to Dix and repeated, "Grandpa says please pass the peas."

"Tell Grandpa," she began, then caught herself and passed the peas instead.

Melissa's chair scraped back on the wood floor.

"Bring me some more ice tea, if you're goin'," Iris ordered from her end of the table.

46

Melissa looked to Dix. Betty's head swiveled from face to face around the table, the baby lurching toward the spoon as it wavered.

"Aw, just siddown," Ed said.

Dix looked down at her plate, then to her father. She met his eyes. "Apologize, Dad," she said.

Ed's face remained studiously blank. He focused his eyes beyond her head. She looked over to Melissa and lifted her shoulders in a shrug. She had tried.

"Wass the matter," Ed said to Melissa, "Can't take a joke?"

Iris rattled the ice in her glass. "Get a move on if you're goin', girl. I'm dry as dust."

Melissa sighed and began to untangle her chair, reaching for the empty pitcher.

"I'll get it." Dix grabbed the pitcher and escaped to the kitchen, smacking the swinging door hard with her palm. The sound was that of a slap.

"Just look at how he follows this spoon," she heard Betty say behind her. "Everybody look." Yeh, everybody look at something besides Dad being an ass, Dix thought. Her hand smarted and the door still whooshed in and out between the two rooms.

Leaning her head against the cool of the refrigerator, Dix forced herself to breathe in deep through her nose and out through her mouth. Sarah's method. If only Sarah's hands were there to rub away the tight spot at the base of her neck.

"I won't cry," she said to the Bless This House magnet below her nose. Sarah would *make* her cry, would wrap her arms around her from behind and hold tight, whispering, "It hurts, it hurts, it hurts," until Dix let the tears come. She bit her lip. "He won't make me cry," she whispered and clenched her fists. "Fucking asshole." Swearing helped. "Stupid fucking asshole," she whispered.

The dining room door creaked on its hinge and Dix straightened up, drawing in her breath. "Bud," she said and let out her breath. "Shit," she said. He grimaced. "Uh, shoot," she corrected herself. "I thought you were Mom." She opened the freezer door and cooled her face as she grabbed the ice.

"Hey, you can't let him get to you." Dix felt his hand, scratchy with calluses, grab her shoulder, and she blinked into the frosty air of the ice box. "Hey, thanks for what you tried to do in there." His hand lifted and fell in a heavy pat.

"Yeah, sure." She held an ice cube in her slightly throbbing hand and turned to her brother. "I just don't think he should get away with that shit — stuff." Buddy shook his head at the word, but she went on. "Why do you let him get away with it? At least Melissa tries to stand up to him. Where the hell were you?"

Bud crossed his arms in front of his chest and rocked back on his heels. "No need for dirty language, Dix." He paused and looked away, out of the kitchen window. "You all just don't understand. I work with him every day. I'm not about to let him get me all riled up about every little thing. Why bother? It's easier to just stay out of the way, you know?" He stared for a minute longer, then shook his head. "Where's that tea?"

He took the pitcher and Dix followed him with the bowl of ice. She wondered if Bud knew from whom he had learned about staying out of the way.

She wondered if she should bother trying to explain why he should bother.

"Shhh, shush ..." The dining room had erupted in an exaggerated hushing. Red and Skeeter, the older boys, puffed out their cheeks with air as if even breathing would allow the secret to escape. They squirmed on their phone books, trying not to grin at their dad. Skeeter couldn't stand it. "Sunday's Father's Day," he shouted.

"Quiet, stupid!" Red tried to kick his brother under the table, sliding down to rest his chin beside his plate to accomplish it.

Iris snorted from her end of the table. The baby looked around and grinned toothlessly while Betty dabbed at the strained peas dribbling from the corner of his mouth. Melissa rolled her eyes at Dix.

"Boys." Bud's voice held a tone of Ed in it. Dix took another look at him as they sat down.

"We were just discussing what the boys were giving their daddy for Father's Day," Betty said. "It's going to be a big surprise, isn't it?" She gave Red and Skeeter one of those looks. "Your daddy and Aunt Dixie always had a big surprise for Grandpa, you know."

Red swiveled in his chair and looked hard at Dix next to him. "Grandpa's your daddy?"

Iris snorted again. "Outa the mouths of babes ..." she muttered.

"Will you just look at the appetite of this child," Betty exclaimed. She and Melissa and Bud chattered on about how much the little one, they were calling him Peanut, could eat.

" 'Bout as round and sweet as a coconut," Iris joined in.

All nuts, Dix thought. Skeeter and his grandpa were playing an intricate game with silverware. Red still stared at Dix.

Finally he leaned over and pulled her ear close to his mouth. "What you gettin' *your* daddy for Father's Day," he said loudly, forgetting to whisper. The table was suddenly quiet.

"All I want for Father's Day," Ed began importantly, voice deepening as he spoke, "is to look down that pew on Sunday mornin' —" He sat back in his chair and swept his arm as if down a row, "and see all my children and grandchildren sittin' there with me before the Lord God." He sat back. "That's the only gift will do." Silence.

Dix felt it swell from the tight spot at the nape of her neck. It rushed through her chest and burst into the dining room before she could stop it. Even Peanut stared, his mouth a toothless Oh, while she laughed, hiccupping through tears. "Sorry, I'm sorry," she babbled, backing out of the dining room, laughing and laughing and laughing.

I *have always been fascinated with point of view. A professor in graduate school once told me he thought I was schizophrenic because I wrote from so many angles so well.*

The schizophrenia used to drive Sarah insane. I would always present the other side of every argument, every trouble she ran into in the world. She wanted me to only see it her way, or, maybe, my way.

I don't really know what my point of view is sometimes. When I came back that summer Grandma died, I was trying to figure it out. I tried to figure out how everyone else was seeing things. Each point of view gave me a different slant on things, and each one seemed to add something important to my perspective.

Now I look back and wonder if that professor was not perhaps partly right. That particular schizophrenia may be part of why I am back now. I want to claim it. All points of view are also my point of view.

Back in this room in my grandmother's house where people go to die, I am the omniscient, the third person, the second, and the first. I am all the others, and I am still only me. I am perhaps schizophrenic because I am trying to understand.

Part Two: Weekend

Friday Is Not the End
of Anything

Jacksonville to Point Will was nothing these days, about as easy as headin' over to the Jiffy Store for a moon pie. Only the scream of his Jackrabbit Radar Detector could keep Ed Major from making the trip to his mama's for dinner in less than forty-four minutes these days. He could drive this stretch of I-95 in his sleep. Of course, if he got a ticket, his whole schedule would be thrown off, not to mention his blood pressure. The problem with the dad-blamed state patrol these days was they were making so much money off selling drug-runners' vehicles they could afford the newest do-dads for catchin' honest citizens runnin' a steady seventy-five like himself.

He was a safe driver, no doubt about it ... said so right on his license. Ed pulled closer to the T-Bird's New Jersey tag. It was characters like this guy — especially Yankees — who made the roads unsafe ... doin' sixty in the runnin' lane, imagine. The eyes of the T-Bird's driver popped wide in the rearview mirror. Ed inched the nose of his Town Car a hair closer to the other guy's bumper. The right turn signal began flashing immediately. Communication, that's what it was all about.

Ed popped in his First Baptist Church Praises tape and settled back into corinthian leather. That Merilee sure could hit the high notes, not like Anita, of course, but he'd had to throw out those tapes when she got her divorce. Just couldn't support that kind of behavior.

Ed's stomach rumbled. Without Betty home to cook, he'd thought he'd lose weight ... he'd counted on it, in fact. But the Jiffy Store and those moon pies were just too easy. And bein' on the road all the time didn't help any. Up to Savannah twice this week already because the inspectors had cited the hole as unsafe ... heck, it was just him and Buddy anyway. They'd got out of that one that caved in over in Tallahassee last week easy enough. Government oughta keep its nose outa a family business. We kin take care of ourselves right enough, he thought, and grinned at the memory of Bud all covered in mud climbin' outa that soup.

His stomach rumbled again. Yep, droppin' in to

Mama's for dinner three or four times a week was the only thing keepin' him going.

The tree farms opened up into the wide expanse of marsh grass which flanked the river separating Florida from Georgia. Wetlands, they called it now. Just meant more permits, more dad-blamed government inspectors lookin' over your shoulder, and more taxes to pay for 'em. Didn't need anybody to watch out for a bunch of marsh grass . . . Why, he'd seen where the nuclear power plant down towards Tampa had actually built 'em back up good as new. Dixie had took 'em to see the manatees at the viewing platform — they liked the warm outflow from the cooling towers — and he'd seen fishermen pulling whoppers out of the water . . . So what if their fins were kind of funny-lookin' and some of 'em didn't have eyes . . . you cut that part off anyway. Why, just like he'd told Dixie, with modern technology and a little old-fashioned ingenuity, most anything can be put back the way it was.

The traffic began to slow around him, but he knew the marked car at the inspection station was just for show. That cop had it easy. He'd sit in the booth and drink coffee until some U-Hauling snowbird who didn't know better bypassed the pull-off, then chase 'em down at a hundred miles an hour, make 'em unload everything on the side of the road lookin' for drugs, and give 'em a five hundred dollar ticket t' boot. He didn't stop at weigh stations much anymore. Since that night that fool tried to cite him for harassment, Buddy drove all the trucks over state lines. They always had it in for the honest businessman.

The rise of the bridge was just ahead. Ed glanced

off toward Roses Bluff about a mile downriver on his right. Amazing nobody had developed it yet. Probably 'cause the clay cliff would keep falling into the river into eternity and 'cause the dad-blamed sand gnats would eat you alive over there — that discouraged folks. Still, there oughta be a way to overcome those drawbacks . . . prime real estate like that.

Just over the bridge, he whipped right past the welcome station, exiting on Point Will Road. Georgia and Florida were pretty much the same, as far as he was concerned . . . except Georgia had a state income tax. He supposed he liked the city life better. Nothin' to stay in Point Will for these days. The narrow blacktop highway passed nothing but pine trees in rows and an occasional tin-roofed shack. He'd bet he'd driven this road a million times. One way into town, one way out, and a dead-end to boot.

Up ahead a small line of cars was braking. What the heck? He couldn't see any pulpwood truck ahead, the usual culprit on this road. The cars began passing into the left lane. An old blue Chevy pickup limped to a stop on the shoulder. Ed's stomach rumbled. Danged rubberneckers were makin' him late to dinner. Mama hated that. Heck, it was just a flat tire.

As he changed lanes, a young woman, hair pulled back in a fiery ponytail, climbed out of the truck, stood by the front left flat and said an obviously dirty word. Ed grinned, then caught himself. Pretty young girl like that usin' that kind of language . . . Of course, he'd used that word himself a time or two . . . just slipped out, of course, like when that weigh station cop had tried to haul him off. The girl kicked the tire hard.

Ed hesitated a second, then flipped on his signal and whipped off onto the shoulder. If that were his own daughter, he'd appreciate some upstanding fellow like himself stoppin' to lend a hand. He shifted into reverse and roared back up the shoulder to the Chevy. You never knew what kind of crazies and perverts were out there. Decent folk had to watch out for each other.

The redhead peered around at him from the back of the truck as he got out of his car. She frowned. A big black Lab stuck his head out the driver-side window and began to bark in serious, slow woofs. Cars whooshed by in regular hot gusts.

"Need some help there, little lady?" he yelled from beside the Town Car. He wasn't gettin' any too close to that dog. He kinda wished Dixie would travel with her dog more often . . . black Lab kind of like that one . . . just for the safety factor. Like this time, he'd heard her tell Betty she'd left the dog home . . . probably with that woman she lived with.

Ed sighed. He couldn't tell that girl anything. Willful, that one. No respect for what was right and decent, no respect for her mama or her daddy. He just couldn't figure how he'd raised such a child. He'd done the best he could, but the devil had got ahold of her some way anyhow.

He sighed again and took a step toward the blue pickup. The dog lunged forward, as if to jump out of the cab.

"Stay! you goof." The woman came around the side of the truck rolling her spare. She stopped and hugged the big, black head, and looked at Ed. The dog gave an obligatory woof. "I can probably handle it myself," she called, and shrugged.

Ed held out his palms. "Just tryin' to be neighborly," he said. "Got a daughter about your age. Know I'd appreciate some other good ole fella helpin' her out."

She was already bent over the flat, hardly glancing at him. The Lab drooled down the driver's door, grinning at Ed. He lifted his shoulders and turned back to the car. Heck, he'd tried. He heard the lug wrench clang on the pavement behind him.

"Hey, mister," she called. Ed turned, standing in the open car door. She started toward him. "I'm sorry, maybe you can help . . . the lug nuts are too tight." She held out the wrench toward him and grinned, shrugging.

"Don't blame ya, don't blame ya a bit," Ed said, slamming the car door and taking the lug wrench from the girl. "You can't be too careful these days, you know." The Lab growled as Ed neared the cab. "Take it easy, boy." Ed walked slowly. "It's okay." The dog cocked his head and lifted his nose to sniff the air. He seemed to frown. "Woof." It had a questioning note, half-hearted.

The woman stood by the window and put her arm around him. "Lota protection you are," she laughed. The dog licked her face sloppily and Ed laughed too. "Usually he's a lot more aggressive than this," she said. "I guess you must be okay."

Ed leaned into the lug wrench and grunted as the nut suddenly loosened. He twirled the wrench nonchalantly, one bolt after another, then jacked the truck the rest of the way up. "Great old rig you got here," he said. "Got a 'thirty-two Pontiac myself . . . made the same year I was born." He chuckled and looked up at her. " 'Course it's been restored . . ." She laughed along, absently stroking her dog's head. "What's this, about a 'fifty-two?" he asked. "Did ya buy it redone or have somebody do it for ya?"

She didn't answer immediately, and Ed looked up from wiggling the flat off the hub. She sure was a pretty one . . . all that red hair and them freckles and blue eyes . . . kinda reminded him of Betty in the old days.

"Yeah, 'fifty-two," the girl answered slowly. "You know your antiques." She was staring at Ed's Lincoln oddly. She leaned out toward the traffic lanes, trying to see the writing on the side of the car.

"Careful there, little lady," Ed said, and she stepped back and watched him roll the spare tire closer. "Nice paint job," he commented.

"Actually, I did the painting myself. You don't think it's too much?"

Ed looked down the side of the truck, royal blue with a narrow flaring racing strip of tiny triangles in pink and light blue all tumbled together in kind of a Z slash. It wasn't gaudy like some of the things you saw on young folks' vehicles these days, in fact you'd hardly notice the detail except as a flared stripe unless you looked close. "Looks okay to me," he said, " 'course I tend to prefer the traditional, you know." He chuckled. "Just an old fogey, I guess."

He tightened the last lug nut and began jacking the truck down. "You did a clean job on it, that's for sure." He really meant the compliment. This was as good as anything he'd seen done in a body shop. He retightened the nuts and hoisted the flat.

She followed him around to the tailgate. "Let's just put it in the back." She dug her key out of her jeans and unlocked the topper.

61

Ed put the tire in, careful not to disturb the equipment bags on the bare bed. The tailgate was decorated with a jumble of large triangles continued from the stripe on the sides. Ed touched the detail, very smooth. He stepped back to read her bumper stickers. About what he'd expected: Greenpeace, ProChoice, No Nukes . . . Too bad, another misguided youngster. He reached for his wallet, then stopped.

"Hey," he said, tapping the sticker in her window, "Bass Association — me too."

The girl pushed a stray strand of hair back from her face and smiled. "Yeah? Know any good spots around here? I'm going to be staying in a little town up the road for a few days. No boat, though."

Ed grinned and reached for his wallet again. "Well, for bass, the St. Johns is good back past Jacksonville a ways, but you'll definitely want to try out the salt water bank fishing if you're gonna be anywhere around here. Just get ya some bait shrimp, ask anybody where. Not bass, but . . ."

He found the slip of paper in his wallet. "Now if you're gonna be around this area on Sunday, I wanna invite ya t' come on back down to my church." He gave her the tract. "We got a full orchestra, real pretty music, lotsa young folks . . . good-lookin' young fellas . . ." He winked. She held the tract between two fingers. "Jacksonville's not a bit far from here . . . directions right on the back."

The girl looked at him funny. "Thank you."

They came around the side of the truck. The dog was watching for them. "Thanks for your help," she said, and stuck out her hand.

"No trouble at all, little lady." Ed brushed his hand on his slacks and shook hers. "Like I said, if my girl was in the same spot, I'd appreciate knowin' some regular old fella like me was stoppin' to help her 'stead 'a some weirdo."

She looked from Ed to the tract, then leaned out, looking toward his car again. She shook her head and put her hand on the door handle.

"You get that tire fixed quick, now, you hear?" he called out, walking toward the car. "Wouldn't want ya ta get stuck without a spare."

He settled into the wide leather seats of his Lincoln and shoved the a.c. to max. The blue pickup pulled out and passed him. The girl waved, looking hard at his door where the company logo was stenciled. She grinned and accelerated ahead.

Nice girl, Ed thought. Respectful, quiet, pretty, long hair. Nice girl. Get her right with God and involved with some good, wholesome right-thinking church activities, she'd meet one of them good Christian fellas.

Ed sighed. All that liberal crap on her bumper. Devil was just havin' his own way in this old world. Baby killers and communists gettin' their hold on all the young folk. His own daughter gone to the perverts, and him an usher in the second biggest church in the South. Signs of the last days. Couldn't have much hope for this old world when your own turned against you just for spite. No wonder they wouldn't make him a deacon. If only Betty hadn't gone to pastoral counseling and spilled the beans. That dirty word popped into Ed's head but he blanked it quick and stomped on the accelerator.

At seventy-five, he had to brake behind the bumper of a U-Hauling Pinto struggling up the incline of a bridge, trying to pass a semi-truck.

Danged snowbirds, move to Florida for five months and twenty-eight days and pay no taxes, how's that fair? What were they doin' on the road to the Point anyway? Maybe weekenders, goin' camping or something. Heck, for a real working man, Friday wasn't the end of anything.

His speedometer was on fifty by the time the Pinto passed in front of the semi. The Town Car roared over the top of the bridge and Ed glared at the two young men in the Pinto as he passed. Probably queers or drug runners, or both, he thought. He yanked right, in front of the small car, and put his foot on the brake pedal. That'll teach 'em. The Pinto swerved, the trailer wagged like a tail as they braked. The semi-truck loomed close and Ed saw the driver reach up to pull the horn one long blast.

Ed grinned and sped easily toward the Welcome to Point Will sign. When he noticed his Jackrabbit Radar Detector screaming, the trooper's car was already in his rearview mirror.

This time Ed said it aloud: "Shit."

*T*he pointer of God. When I finally got to the Sistine Chapel a couple of years ago, tired and sweaty and smelly from days of hosteling and hitching and train travel, I stood there and tilted my neck back with all the other tourists and immediately thought of my father's index finger. My hand actually clenched in a fleeting muscle memory of reaching far far up to hold onto that finger as we walked into the church. Now here was God reaching out to Adam, limp, like my dad had once reached out to me. I felt *completely alien suddenly — completely alone in the world.*

Here, writing in this room, Iris gone, Sarah gone, the family gone, no one home, I think suddenly: I am alone at the Point. Then the mailman rattles the box or a car crunches on the coquina shell drive or a cardinal calls out to his mate, and my feeling of being an alien evaporates. I am at the Point.

He was the Father. He modeled himself after the Father, and the Father was modeled after him. As I grew closer in height to the pointer of God, he withdrew from me. Perspective is tricky.

That summer when Iris died, that time I am trying to put into perspective, his silence was as loud as the silence of God. He heard, but he did not speak, as if I were praying to him. Was I praying to him? I did not bother to speak to his God; I haven't for years. When I speak to those who do not answer, is it truly my prayer?

I read, and I believe, that silence is lying. It is a refusal to acknowledge the existence of something or someone. Our silences were complex that summer. Our lies were thick as the air at noon. Was my silence to Grandma any less than Dad's to me?

The pointer of God. I wandered the Sistine Chapel, all alone in the world, until I found Adam and Eve being banished forever from the Garden. It struck me then. Pointing in accusation looks a lot like reaching out for a little girl's grasp.

Don't They Burn Witches?

The house was just as Dix had described it. Sarah would have recognized it anywhere.

She had suspected her lover of idealizing the house and Point Will along with the rest of her childhood summers here. Dix had to have exaggerated the eccentricities of her family; Sarah figured nobody's family was as bad as they imagined, not that she would know, of course, never having had any real family herself. But this house and this town did look like old South, small town America, exactly as Dix had said. This is the old South, Sarah reminded herself; a picture-pretty gray stone house, moss-draped trees, a stifling, silent heat.

She pulled onto the lawn at the edge of the street. No need for sidewalks here, she thought, this was the kind of place where everyone walked down the middle of the road, kind of slow.

Dawg whined out the window at a ragged collie lying in the dirt driveway across the street. "Okay, okay." Sarah shoved the dog back and opened her door. He jumped out and got right to the business of smelling trees. She stood by her truck and looked around.

The house was square, made of some kind of rectangular gray stones. The porches, upstairs and down, and the trim around the tall windows, a balanced two on either side of the doors both upstairs and down, were painted a slightly peeling white. The even weight appealed to Sarah's eye, and she liked the way the jasmine trellis on one end of the porch offset the swing hanging from chains on the other end. A half-dozen mismatched rocking chairs faced the street or each other in random groups. The whole scene was framed by the two trees on either side of the walk — she smelled bay — and a white shell drive on the left, and wisteria-draped cedar trees on the right. Nice picture, but dull, she thought. Too nice. A good picture needed some drama.

"No fair!" screamed a kid from the yard off to the right of the house. "Red, wait!" A hedge of azalea bushes screened the voices from Sarah's view, but they were headed her way.

"Slowpoke," the leader taunted. "You baby!" A tall boy, maybe six or so and crowned with an unruly shock of red hair, trotted backwards from behind the hedge. "You're just a baby!" he sing-songed, turning to sprint ahead as he cleared the hedge into the front yard.

When he saw Sarah, he stopped short. Another little boy, also redheaded but stockier and perhaps a year younger, cleared the hedge at a full run, and smashed into his brother, toppling both to the ground.

"Gotcha," he crowed between gasps, "I gotcha!"

"Knock it off, you butt-head," the bigger boy said. "Look."

They both lay in the grass, staring at Sarah. She stood with her arms crossed, still leaning against the pickup.

"Who that?" the little one asked.

"Shut up."

Obviously Dix's nephews, Sarah thought. Looked a lot like Betty, anyway. They were dirty, in that little kid way, but basically your average kids.

Dawg ambled back across the street from his visit with the collie and saw the kids in the grass. His tail waved and he trotted toward them.

"Doggie!" the smaller boy shouted and scrambled off his brother's back. Red got to his feet more slowly, but he was smiling.

"No!" Sarah heard Dix's mother's scream from the side of the house. "Skeeter, no!" There was a note of hysteria in her voice. "Stay away from that dog! Red, stop him!" Betty appeared running, head down, a dishtowel clutched in one hand.

Sarah grinned. Dawg and Skeeter continued jogging in slow-motion toward each other, both looking dopey, both drooling, and Sarah thought of a toothpaste commercial, a love-at-first-sight scene. Red still stared at her. Betty ran with her head down.

"Betty!" she called.

Betty's head tilted just slightly, but she pounded down the lawn.

"Betty!" Sarah pushed herself off the truck and started forward.

Betty made the full turn, then jerked back in a double take.

"Ahh," Betty said, looking from Sarah to Skeeter and Dawg exchanging kisses and back. The dishtowel dropped from her hand. "Ahhh." She sank to the grass. "Land sakes, you scared the livin' daylights outa me."

"You okay, Grandma?" Red asked.

Betty nodded, panting. "Go on, I'm fine, honey." She found her dishtowel and dabbed at her brow. "All I could think when I saw that big ole black dog was of little Shirley Weldon and the terrible mess that German shepherd made of her face. Poor little thing, she never did get over it."

Sarah reached down to give Betty a hand up. Betty said, "Grew up and moved to New York City, you know."

Sarah hoisted her up, and Betty stood holding both her hands for a minute. "How *are* you dear? Boys, don't fight over that dog, now, he's big enough for both of you."

Dawg fell over good-naturedly as both the kids tried to sit on him. "Aren't they just a mess?" Betty twisted the dishtowel in her hands. "Now tell me how you *are*," she said.

Sarah smiled. Betty was something else. "Fine, just fine," she began.

"Boys, don't do that." Betty shook her head and frowned. "He might not like that." Dawg shook the hands off his nose and sneezed.

"Yuck!" Red wiped his arm on his brother, who pushed back. Dawg snuffled into their wrestling match and sneezed again.

"Boys!" Betty warned. "How was your trip?" she continued, crossing her arms, frowning suddenly up the street.

"Okay," Sarah said, following her gaze, "except I had a flat just outside town."

The street was empty, shadowy with oaks and moss, but Betty continued to look, worriedly. Sarah knew she was watching for Dix's dad, Ed. She'd recognized the Major Construction logo on the side of the car after he'd helped with the tire. Betty seemed distracted; Sarah couldn't decide whether it would be better to tell her she'd met Ed or not.

She watched the tiny lines at the corners of Betty's mouth. Dix's mom was an attractive woman, pale freckles, salt-and-pepper permed hair, rounded but not overweight. Her eyes were the same as Dix's, emerald green, but no one had Dix's lashes. Sarah looked back down the side of the house and across the front porch, expecting to see her appear. No one.

"I did get some help changing it — the tire — so it wasn't so bad," Sarah finished.

Betty looked over quickly, frowning. "Oh, I worry so about you young girls traveling alone. Was it a man? I just wouldn't let anyone near me on the side of a road like that. I've tried and tried to get Dixie to get Triple-A. That man who sold it to me just told the most awful stories. Why even the police . . . There was a woman over in Alabama was found dead and

71

all chopped up in the woods, and do you know, it was the very policeman who stopped to help her that had done it. You can't trust anybody these days."

She shook her head, wrapping and unwrapping the dishtowel from her hands. "If I was to have a flat tire, I'd just lock all the doors and sit there until someone stopped and give them a quarter to call Triple-A without rolling my window down or anything . . . not even a policeman —"

A scream interrupted her. "Boys, behave."

"Hey." Sarah felt the light touch on the back of her arm and smelled Dix at the same moment. She smiled and turned and pulled the familiar form into a hug.

Dix was stiff, didn't give, but Sarah held her close, touched the back of her lover's neck, then spread her palm to hold the clenched muscle there. Let go, Sarah thought, relax. She pressed her lips gently to the skin between nape and T-shirt — the place where my heart lives, she always told Dix — and finally Dix's hands softened and spread at the base of her spine.

"Hey yourself," Sarah said softly, and they pulled apart.

Red stood, feet apart, arms crossed, staring frankly at them. "Who you?" Skeeter asked. Sarah opened her mouth.

"You boys need to get washed up for dinner," Betty said to them. Red continued to stare, and Dix dropped Sarah's hand.

Skeeter leaned both his arms on Dawg's back and clasped his hands. "Who you?" he demanded more loudly.

Sarah stuck out her hand to Skeeter. "I'm Sarah. Charmed, I'm sure."

Skeeter took her hand, then twisted back and pointed at the design on her truck. "Zorro!" he shouted.

Betty laughed. "Too many old movies with Grandpa."

"Zorro," Skeeter repeated, shaking Sarah's hand vigorously.

"Okay, if you insist," she laughed. "Zorro. Now," she added, "who you?"

Skeeter shook firmly one more time, took a deep breath, and announced, "Paul Jefferson Major."

"Aw, he's just Skeeter," his brother said in a rush. "He don't know anything. He's just a baby."

"Peter and Paul, better known as Red and Skeeter," Dix said, smiling.

Betty dabbed at her brow with her dishtowel and looked up the street. "Better wash up, boys," she repeated. "You know how Granny likes dinner on time." She glanced up as Sarah reached over and touched Dix's arm. She grasped a little boy firmly with each hand. "Now," she said. She marched them toward the back of the house amid choruses of "aw."

Dix turned to Sarah. "Don't push it," she said. Her eyes were brilliant and hard.

Nobody had those lashes, Sarah thought. "I'm not going to let you get away," she answered. She nodded toward the house. "And I'm not going to let you get away with hiding behind all this." She heard the Lincoln with Major Construction stenciled on the door rumbling up the shadowy street. "You can't let them get away with it, and you know it."

"Let's not make it worse than it is," Dix said, so close Sarah could feel the heat of her breath. She knew Dix didn't see her dad's car. Sarah smiled, reached out and pulled the long body to her, hands firmly against the back of her neck, and kissed her, holding on until Dix's mouth softened and the nape of neck ceased its strain back and settled into Sarah's hands. Now *this* will put some drama in the picture, she thought.

"Out, I want her out, now!"

Sarah heard Ed's voice. She stood a step lower than Dix on the back stoop. Dix's hand was on the door, but she didn't go in. Her dad's voice kept rising, and her mom's kept shushing it.

"I don't care how you explain it to Mama, I want them out of this house."

Sarah smiled at the back pockets of Dix's jeans. This should be interesting.

"Right out there on the street where anybody can see. Pure evil. People in this town know .me."

So this was the infamous Ed. Not exactly the good old boy who had changed her tire. He was nice enough when he wanted to be, Sarah thought. Fathers were a complete mystery to her, and Dix's experience with this one had done nothing to make them any clearer.

His voice went suddenly just a little softer. "Don't want nothin' to happen."

Was he worried about Dix or himself? Sarah

reached out and touched the back of Dix's thigh. Dix jumped away startled, looked back and scowled. "I told you," she warned softly.

Sarah shrugged. Yeah, she'd already gotten the lecture after Ed's Lincoln had spun shells all the way up the driveway. For Grandma, Dix had said, for me. Sarah wondered about that. Did Dix really know what *for me* was? She didn't want to make Dix too angry, but maybe it was time she faced things — her family — more directly.

"I'm sure Dixie will behave," Betty said. "None of us want to make this time hard on your mother." Ed's voice grumbled. "Don't worry," Betty said. "Just try to be nice, dear."

"Humph." Sarah couldn't help muttering it. *Too* nice, that was the problem

Dix gave her another look and opened the screen door.

A stairway rose up from the kitchen entry, and Sarah saw Red's face at the top. She winked at him and he disappeared. Dix stood in the doorway, and Sarah brushed past her into the kitchen.

"Hi."

Betty stood by the sink, her hands wrapped in the dishtowel. Deep furrows channeled between Ed's eyes as he recognized her from the roadside.

Dix cleared her throat. "Um, Sarah, this is my dad. Dad, Sarah."

Ed stood silent, hands clenched on the edge of the butcher block in the center of the room.

Sarah stepped forward, hand stuck out, smiling. "We've already met." She grabbed Ed's hand off the counter. He took a minute to react, then drew it back while she continued, "Mr. Major was kind enough to help me change a flat."

Ed tried to keep his face blank, but the lines between his brows furrowed deeper. Sarah wondered if he would speak to her, or if she was to receive the silent treatment like Dix. "I guess this was one man it was okay to trust on the side of the road," she said.

Betty opened her mouth, then closed it. Ed crossed his arms over his chest and turned his back to leave.

Sarah swallowed. "Mr. Major, is there a good place to get my flat fixed around here?" she asked.

Ed walked away without answering. Sarah glanced at Dix and saw the frown. She needs to see what her dad does to her, Sarah thought, how hard it really is. She inhaled. "Too bad about that ticket, huh?" she called.

Dix groaned. Sarah turned to Betty who was staring down at the bowl of peas on the counter. You *should* be embarrassed, Sarah thought. *I* am, we *all* are, letting him get away with it. She sighed into the silence and kitchen heat. "What can I do to help?" she finally asked.

A voice from the next room called, "It's nearly twelve-thirty, get a move on, I'm about to perish in here."

Betty looked up. A quick frown flashed over her face. "Dix, will you take these peas in? I'll find the boys." She turned, then stopped and turned back to Sarah. "I know you're a nice girl, dear." She touched Sarah's arm. "Dixie's grandmother is in very poor health, and I know you won't want to upset her any

76

more than the rest of us do." She smiled weakly, and Sarah watched her scurry into the living room.

"So Betty's your referee, eh?" she said to Dix.

Dix set the bowl of peas down hard on the counter. "Just stop it," she hissed. "This is not a fucking game — it's my life. Don't make it worse than it already is."

They stared at each other for a second, then Dix shook her head. "Shit." She sank into a chair and massaged her brow. "Why did you even come here? What the hell do you want?" She looked up into Sarah's eyes. "What is this going to accomplish?"

"I —" Sarah began.

"Listen, I'm leaving," Dix said. "You know I'm leaving in the fall. I've got to go. I've got to do this. I love you, but I have to go and give myself a chance."

Sarah opened her mouth, but Dix wasn't looking at her. "I wish we could be together, but we can't," she said, her tone one of recitation.

Let her say it one more time, Sarah thought.

"You've just got to understand," Dix said, "it's just not going to work. Just let it end." She put her hands around the bowl of peas. "Please leave me alone," she said softly, looking into the steam rising off the vegetables.

Sarah let the silence settle into the kitchen. That had been a tough one for Dix, she knew. Confronting was something Dix had had to learn, had had to learn that it was not going to drown love out, had had to learn it from her. Sarah's eyes stroked the curve of her lover's back up to her neck to the dark head bent into the warm mist from the bowl.

As she reached out, Dix pushed back from the

77

table and stood up with the peas, still staring down. Voices echoed in from the dining room. As Dix's body brushed her own in the tight spot past the refrigerator, Sarah placed her hand on the curve of her neck. She held it for a second and put her mouth close to Dix's ear.

"No," she whispered, then let her pass into the dining room.

"Land sakes, I just can't get over Ed bein' the one to stop and fix your tire." Dix's grandmother grinned down from the head of the table. She basically controlled things, Sarah guessed, though she did seem to run out of breath regularly, settling back into the wooden armchair to breathe and watch with those cool gray eyes. She was a tiny woman, but her gaze was sharp and commanding. "Son, can you get over that?"

"No, Mama." Ed was a sullen weight at the opposite end of the long table. Sarah had the feeling he wasn't usually this quiet. Red and Skeeter were kicking each other under the table, and Betty, across from Sarah, was shoveling food into the baby's face, eyes darting from one face to another. Bud, the brother, kept looking up at her with shy grins, but he didn't speak except to ask her to pass this or that. Melissa, the wife, with luxurious dark curls framing a sweet oval face, sat on the other side of Bud and kept her lips tight together and avoided Sarah's eyes. Dix watched her plate mostly.

Sarah looked back at Iris. "Oh, I think

coincidences happen more than we realize, we just don't always notice."

Iris grinned. "Oh, I know my boy," she said. "Stoppin' to help a pretty young thing like you warn't no coincidence."

Ed frowned and sat back in his chair. "Just bein' neighborly," he muttered.

"And I do thank you, Mr. Major," Sarah said. He looked at her. "I'd probably still be fighting that lug wrench." The table was very quiet.

"Welcome," Ed finally said.

Dix looked up slowly at her father, continuing to stare as Betty began chattering to the baby and Ed asked Bud about the job in Brunswick. So she sees, Sarah thought, watching her lover's green eyes, wide under the dark lashes.

Iris touched her arm and began describing the places Sarah would want to photograph in Point Will. "I want you to know you're welcome to stay as long as you want," she said. She touched Sarah's arm. "Dixie's friends are always welcome in my house."

Sarah looked over to Dix, but she was still staring at her father. As Sarah watched, Dix straightened her shoulders, leaned across Skeeter and said in a slow, loud, deliberate voice, "Dad, will you please pass the cornbread?"

"So you got to dig that hole about five feet deeper on account 'a that gas line is off the center." As Ed continued talking, everyone else stopped.

"Dad, may I please have the cornbread?" Dix repeated.

Ed leaned toward the windows. "Might rain early today," he said.

Sarah watched Dix swallow hard and felt it in her own throat.

"Dad," Dix began again.

"Land sakes alive," Iris shouted down the table. "You goin' deef already, boy? Pass that girl some cornbread."

Ed picked up the basket and handed it to Skeeter.

"Must be gettin' old or somethin'," Iris muttered to herself, "own son losin' his hearin'."

Sarah felt Red squeeze in between her and his dad. "Now you will stay with us for awhile, won't you Sarah?" Iris asked. Sarah felt Red tapping on her arm. "How long did you say you could visit?"

"Hey," Red interrupted.

Sarah put her hand on his arm and answered Iris. "I'm pretty flexible, Mrs. Major," she said. "At least through the weekend, though." She glanced down the table to Ed. "I've been invited to church Sunday over in Jacksonville."

Dix's mouth dropped open.

"Hey," Red repeated, shaking her arm now. "Hey."

Sarah turned her full attention on him. "Hey," she said back. "What?"

He looked at her seriously. "Granpa says," he labored out the words. "Granpa says you're evil." He stopped in the table silence, then tumbled on. "Is you a witch?"

Sarah looked slowly over Red to Dix, who rolled her eyes to the ceiling. No one moved. At the far end of the table, Ed calmly lifted his fork to his mouth and began to chew.

Sarah continued to watch him as she spoke, clearly and slowly. "Why no, Red. You remember, I'm Zorro, the gay blade."

Ed's peas spewed back onto his plate.

I realized as I was unpacking that the only picture of Sarah I had brought back to the Point was a tiny newspaper clipping. After I had settled into my old room, set up my desk and computer here, and dusted mantels and mowed the grass, I took the clipping down to the drugstore and asked the fellow to have it enlarged for me. It took a week, of course; things are still a bit slow at the Point.

I stopped to get the enlargement on my evening walk yesterday. I waited amid all the things only *grandmothers need: plastic rain hats, bobby pins, emery boards, Maalox. I remembered shopping here for Grandma that summer, filling her prescriptions and buying the blue shampoo to keep her curls silver. I bought a bottle for old times' sake, and for my own newly bleached white flat-top. The bottle was dusty, and I wonder how long the Point will stay alive when there are no longer grandmothers to shop at Green's Pharmacy.*

At the landing over the river, I sat down and opened the photo. Sarah. Zorro. The gay blade. I smiled. I am smiling now, looking at her as I write.

The enlarged picture of her is like a pointillist painting, a pattern of dots which do not make sense, except, like an impressionist work, from a distance.

I have framed it.

Friday Night:
Date Night

"And this is the stop sign." Dix grabbed the thin metal sheet of the sign and leaned her head in the crook of her elbow so she could look at Sarah sideways. Zorro. Sarah's camera as her mask. Dix smiled at her. Red-brown curls had worked loose from Sarah's ponytail and blew across her full lower lip. The dusk sky was reflected, blue, but one shade lighter, in her eyes... eye. Sarah squinted and snapped.

"Pretty." Sarah grinned and twisted to glance over her shoulder, back up Main Street, her tank top gaping open at the back, freckles winking at Dix.

Dix's right hand clenched the cool metal tighter, and she brought the other around to hold the base of the sign as well. Keep them anchored so they won't reach out, she thought. A twisting auburn curl danced in the breeze, beckoning, and Dix allowed her eyes to taste the soft freckled expanse of back between Sarah's shoulder blades. Dix licked her suddenly dry lips. No. Only the eyes, she thought, the metal sign sweaty under her palms. No touching. She wants commitment, and I can't. Dix closed her eyes to the sharp, sweet angles of skin. And I'm mad at her, Dix reminded herself. The lights glittered like freckles inside her dark lids . . . Damn. How can I still want her this much?

Dix turned her forehead into the warm crook of her elbow and tried to slow her heart rate. Shit. I don't want this now. I'm not ready. Peace, simplicity, she chanted in her head. Not love, not now.

She heard Sarah's camera click again, and the mewing of gulls, and the whisper of tide and wind in the marsh grasses. Shrimp boats creaked against each other and the dock; water flapped in abrupt, uneven waves against wood. Sarah at the Point, her dad at the Point, Iris dying . . . it wasn't a simple place anymore. Was there any peace left to be found at the Point? Had she ever really found it here anyway?

The scent of Sarah's spicy sweat wrapped around her with the long bare arms. Dix's thighs rocked easily back into the soft form; her stomach muscles contracted in the flat of her lover's palms. The collar of her T-shirt tugged back and Sarah's mouth pressed into her spine, lips then teeth then tongue. "Ummm." Maybe this was peace.

Dix let her head fall back, eyes still closed. On the salt breeze, soft curls draped themselves around her neck, tickling, then breath at her hairline and Sarah's hands pulling in.

"No." Dix snapped straight and tried to pull away. This was the middle of town. Stop, she told herself.

Sarah held her by the armpits, grinned and bit her neck. "Hey."

Hey!" Dix pulled away in a jerk as Sarah goosed her.

Stumbling away, laughing, Sarah reaching out, Dix ducked her hand once, spun and tripped on the lip of the dock just as the other woman's hand grasped hers. They both rocked over into the marigolds the Point Will Beautification Society planted in front of the pavilion each year. For a second they gasped, laughing, in squashed marigold pungency, locked by one hand, watching each other laugh, until it slowed and stopped and the lines of their mouths became still. Sarah's escaping hair was littered with orange-yellow petals.

I want to remember her like this, Dix suddenly thought, and the thought caved in a place below her ribs.

"Fall down, go boom?" Both heads jerked up to the small voice. Skeeter stood with his hands in the bib of his overalls, looking worried. "Okay?" he asked.

His mother loomed up behind him, dark in the fading light, and Red held the straining Dawg by the collar. Dix scrambled to her feet and stood brushing the dirt from her legs. "Just goofing around," she muttered to Melissa.

Sarah leaned up to a seat in the flowers and reached out her hands for a boost. Dix tried to see Melissa's face in the shadows, keeping her hands busy with the dirt on her jeans.

"Ahem," said Sarah.

Red looked up at the other women, one to the other, then let go of the dog and grabbed one of her hands. Skeeter took the other, and with a grunt they hauled Sarah up.

"Don't know how things are down there in your part of the state," Melissa said slowly, "but we keep our private lives private in the South."

All Dix could see was a black gleam where her sister-in-law's eyes were. She was sorry. She and Melissa had been almost close, almost friends, before. When Buddy married young, Dix had known it was a mistake, a mistake for Melissa, but she liked her for being a no-shit girl, for standing up to Ed, for being, even then, the daughter Betty really wanted. Dix supposed she was grateful for that. Then she and John had broken up for good, then she had kept her silence, her private life private, and they had almost been close. Dix thought they were. And then she told Melissa the truth, told her she was going to tell the family she was lesbian. And Melissa told her to keep the silence, keep the family together, keep peace. Dix was sorry.

"I'm sorry," she said.

"Oh, come on!" Sarah spluttered. "What kind of shit is that?"

Melissa's mouth dropped open, and she pulled the boys' heads to her hips, covering their ears.

"Sorry?" Sarah wrapped her palm around the back of Dix's neck, blue eyes six inches away, and softened her voice. "Sorry?" she asked quietly. "Tell me how sorry."

Dix let go, let the warm hand in her hair pull her in and her own hands rest in their natural nook at Sarah's waist, and kissed her. *I am sorry* echoed in Dix's mouth, and she let herself be lost for one peaceful long minute in the whisper of tide in marsh grass, gulls crying, Sarah. I am sorry, she thought.

She watched Melissa march away down Main Street, both boys twisting at the ends of her arms to look back. She waved, smiling and frowning both, over Sarah's shoulder. "Now we've done it," she said, and leaned her forehead on the bare shoulder and blinked at Sarah's blurred freckles. "It doesn't matter." She rolled her head back and forth. "It doesn't matter."

"Bullshit," Sarah said calmly, held her tight a moment then pushed her back. "It matters." She held Dix's gaze. "That's why you're here now. The Point means something to you. This is your family. They matter."

Placing a hand on either side of Dix's face, Sarah stopped her as she began to shake her head no. "What matters more is that you can't choose for them. You can only take care of you. Be you."

Her hands softened and her thumbs smoothed back Dix's temples. "You are beautiful. Let them choose to love you on your terms, or not. Let them go, Dix." Sarah kissed her cheek gently, and Dix felt small and young and loved.

She swallowed the sad, and let her head thump back to Sarah's shoulder. "Shit."

She thought for a minute: the Point, the family, Sarah. Does she think if I let them go, I won't let her go? Can I? Do I want to? She wanted to ask, but instead she just sighed. "You're making this awfully hard for me, you know."

Sarah nudged her nose into the curve of Dix's shoulderblade, and pushed her chin up with her head. She grinned and a few tiny lines fanned out from her eyes. "Yep," she said.

It was good to hold Sarah's hand, but Dix felt a twinge of guilt; the neighbors stared from the front porches as they walked along River Street. She could feel their eyes in the dusk. Ed would have a hard time living this down. Betty would worry that Iris would hear, too. The hand was safe, though. She didn't let it drop. She'd been holding it too long to stop for the Point gossips now.

"So, you got the loans for school," Sarah said. "And maybe the fellowships, as well. The longer they delay on that, the better."

They walked in slow silence, Dawg nosing ahead or behind in the bushes, down-river between marsh and the tin-roofed stilt houses rehabbed in pastels and shutters, then right onto Cemetery Lane. Dix thought maybe she had walked this route a thousand times in her life. Even after she moved west, then down to St. Pete, she found that she often walked these familiar roads, or ran them, in dreams. When she finally did come out to her mom, it had been on this path, just beyond the wall there, in the cemetery. She had written a coming-out story about that day, and it had been published; it had pushed her toward graduate school. I guess I have a lot of stories, she thought, scuffing the gravel, brushing at the *zee* of a mosquito. They've given me stories. Maybe that's why they matter.

They leaned against the rough wall of coquina, gray and worn, and looked over at tilting headstones and weeds and Spanish moss hanging like old women's shawls in a fading light. Sarah squinted at her light meter and shook her head. "Maybe," she murmured. She tried another spot, then another, looking up, looking at her meter, cocking her head at the view. She took a few shots. "I'll definitely want to come back here," she said, then looked up and around the horizon. "What's the moon, now?"

Dix shrugged. "Grandma might know." She smiled into the dark. "Cap would've known for sure, and Aunt Rose, too. You know, Iris's sister. I've told you about her."

Sarah shook her head and shifted her bag behind her back. "No, I don't think I've heard any Aunt Rose stories." She boosted herself up onto the wall beside Dix, and they leaned back to back. "Tell me that story, Dix."

Dix smiled off into the darkness. Sarah had said those words on their first date. She let her head fall back against the soft mat of curls and looked up at the outlines of oaks against space blue. Stories: Sarah had said she didn't have any, matter-of-factly, on that date, but Dix knew better. Sarah had been a foster kid, shuttled from house to house, family to family — her mom had disappeared into the west — and Dix loved those stories. They weren't so tangled up. Sarah had neat beginnings and endings: one year here, four months there, no muddled histories, no real attachments to distract you.

But Sarah wanted Dix's stories. She paid close attention, working out relationships, asking questions to fill in the gaps... "Now she was Iris's stepmother, right? Your dad was the middle kid? Where did they meet? When?" Dix recited for her and heard Iris's echo, Betty's echo, Ed's echo in her own voice. Sometimes the details surprised her; sometimes she wondered how she had pieced together such an intricate quilt. All of that spring Sarah had drawn the stories out. "Tell me that story, Dix, tell me."

"Aunt Rose," she began. "Aunt Rose was Iris's sister, remember?"

"Right," Sarah said, and Dix could feel the smile through her spine. "The flower sisters: Iris, Rose, Violet, Daisy, and Lily. Your great-granddad must have been quite a romantic."

"More of a scoundrel, the way I hear it," Dix replied. "Of course, who knows. People died young back then. So what, he married three teenagers. Not much else he could have done with all those kids to take care of, I suppose. They say Aunt Rose never did quite see it that way, though. Oldest daughter, you know... her stepmothers probably weren't much older than her." Dix smiled at the darkness for a second. Kind of like my own stepkids, she thought, John's kids.

"Anyway, Aunt Rose." She stopped and thought how to begin. A mockingbird started in on a fierce song off among the graves and oaks, and a screen door slammed down the street. "Every Southern family has a tough old bird," Dix began. "That was Aunt Rose. She lived to be ninety-two and managed to insult every person she ever met." Sarah's laugh was low and warm through her back. "The thing was, her insults were simple, brutal truth. She said it like it was, cut through the shit. Social grace was definitely not her forte.

"When she met Melissa the first time, she turned to Bud and said, 'You shore do like 'em big, don't you?' When she met John, she looked him up and down, then said to me, 'An old man gen'erly does make a better husband.'

"She drove this golf cart around town most of the years I remember her. They wouldn't give her a driver's license anymore, probably because the last time she went for the test she said to the lady at the DMV, 'You shore do look like a feller in that get-up.' She said it like it was. They finally put her in a home when she crashed her golf cart.

"Anyway, Cap died, and I came home for the funeral. They wheeled old Aunt Rose into the cemetery, and after the service I went up to say hello, expecting the same old insults, the same old Aunt Rose. I mean everyone else was pretty pissed off at me anyway, since I had just come out to them, and I was wearing my hair spiked up, bleached white, feeling cocky and pretending to be very cool, so there was plenty to target. I was also happy. I felt like I had suddenly met my own self for the first time. I wasn't hiding from me anymore.

"So it was this gorgeous August morning, everybody fanning themselves like mad, Dad already in his car with the a.c. going, Mom holding Iris's hand, everybody basically ignoring me, and there's Aunt Rose spitting chewing tobacco into this jelly jar. I went over and introduced myself to her. 'Now which one are you?' she says. 'Ed's girl.' And I remember standing there, grinning, just waiting for the zinger, and do you know what she did? She looked at me for a long minute and said, 'Ed's girl? Well, I declare.'" Dix heard the twang of Aunt Rose in her voice and smiled to herself. "'Well, I declare,' she said, 'you shore did grow up to be a beauty, didn't you?'"

Dix stopped and felt the catch of hot air in her throat the same as that August morning. "I nearly fell over," she said. "It was the only compliment I ever heard Aunt Rose give in my life."

Sarah's arms reached around backward and hugged her. "She saw right through the shit."

Dix leaned back in the armchair and relaxed into the steady surf-sound of Iris's snore. Seeing through the shit, she thought. Maybe that's why I love Sarah.

She yawned and the cuckoo clock on the stairs echoed three o'clock. Sarah staring Ed down flashed into Dix's memory and she smiled. Not only does she see through it, Dix thought, she confronts it. Am I learning that from her? I should have been the one to say what she said to Mom last night.

They had been sitting in the dark on the front porch, silent in the whir of cicada song, the rocking chairs creaking woodenly, the mosquitoes and sand gnats mercifully kept still by the soft breeze. The giggles of Red and Skeeter splashing through their bath in the old claw foot tub kept Dix's hand from Sarah's until Betty had trooped the boys out for a good-night kiss, then off to bed. The rockers evened pace. Dix felt Sarah's fingers vine into her own like the jasmine on the trellis behind them. They slowed, knitted hands on the armrests, and leaned together to kiss. Dix tasted the jasmine and wisteria of the night on Sarah's breath, laced red hair between her fingers, and let herself be lost in the night sounds.

"Oh, Dixie!"

The screen slammed punctuation behind Betty, and they started up. Betty stood with her hands over her mouth like the shocked heroine in a melodrama, and Dix was torn between a rush of adolescent caught-in-the-yellow-porch-light-guilt and the urge to giggle at her mother's expression. When Sarah laughed aloud, the giggles spluttered out.

Betty's face became suddenly stiff. "Well, I never," she said.

"Oh, sure you did!" Sarah crowed. Dix tried to choke back the laughter gurgling up her chest, but it coughed its way out in spite of her. "Front porches are notorious for this sort of thing. Don't tell me you and Ed never got caught smooching out here."

Dix watched her mother's face work between expressions: adult stern, the soft edges of nostalgia, a fan of smile lines at her eyes. "Come on, Mom, own up," she said.

Betty scowled. "Your father would never approve of such a thing in public. He's a very modest man. You know that, Dixie."

"Some other man, eh," murmured Sarah.

"And I don't approve either. You disappoint me, both of you."

" 'You disappoint me' . . . a mother's big guns, eh," Sarah said.

Dix felt the twinge those "big gun" words were meant to inspire. "Damn it, Mom," she burst out, "that's not fair." She felt her throat constrict but kept on. "I'm not doing anything wrong. Why do you want me to feel bad?" She gulped a breath of jasmine and coughed. Shit.

Betty's lips drew a thin line. Sarah's fingers touched the tips of Dix's own. "I won't be able to sit up with your grandmother tonight, Dixie. You'll have to do it." Betty's voice was prim. She wouldn't meet Dix's eyes.

"Hey," Sarah spoke up. "This is because of me, isn't it?" Her eyes widened in an instant. "Hey, you just don't want anybody sneaking into anybody else's bed, do you?" She leaned her face close to Betty's "Why don't you just say it instead of waltzing around, Mrs. M.?"

"I just don't feel well, Dixie." Betty looked past Sarah to her daughter. "I didn't think you'd mind."

"Why not just say, 'Dixie, don't sleep with your lover,' Betty?" Sarah's voice grew steadier and lower as she spoke. "Why not, 'Don't make love with that woman?' " Dix stopped her with a hand on her arm. Sarah shook her head slowly. "I thought you liked me, Mrs. M. I thought you wanted us to be happy." She glanced at Dix's hand, touched it with the tips of her fingers, then looked into her eyes and shook her head. "I do love you, Dix, whether they do or not. I don't really know what family is, but I'd like to think it's people who want you to be happy, no matter what. I want you to be happy, with me or without me, and with or without your family, but I can't make you be happy, and I don't want you to think you have to choose between us."

She paused. "I'm going to bed." She raised Dix's hand to her lips, squeezed it and opened the screen door.

"Oh, by the way." Sarah glanced at Betty, then grinned, "I'll leave the door unlocked."

The pages of the paperback thumbed softly against Dix's palm. Iris groaned and rolled over heavily, drawing into a tight knot, her hand clenched close to her mouth. How much of that might Grandma have heard, Dix wondered.

She and her mother had stood in the pool of porch light for a long minute while Sarah's steps diminished up the stairs. "I don't mind sitting with Grandma tonight," she had said softly, thinking even now that she did, though. The evening, the walk to the docks, storying on the cemetery wall, kissing on the front porch — it had been almost like a date, a Friday night date. She smiled. Too good to end with sitting up with a sick grandmother, she thought. But she'd said she'd do it anyway, wanting to make Mom feel better, and never mind how she herself felt. Shit. Just what she was trying not to do anymore. Just the sort of thing Betty would have done.

The cuckoo clock squawked once for the half hour in the stairwell. Swallowing hard, Dix remembered that Betty had touched her back as she passed from the porch into the front hall. "I do love you," her mother had murmured.

"Uhnn." Iris grimaced in her sleep and her body flinched tighter for an instant.

Dix sat on the bed's edge and rubbed the nylon-smooth small of Iris's back in wide circles. What was she dreaming? Dix catalogued through the stories she had filed away all those summers with her grandmother. How many more there must be that she had not heard.

Iris started again, and her mouth twisted. "Grandma?" Dix spoke low into her grandmother's ear, then kissed the soft thin skin, pulsing with blue veins like a baby bird's, at her temple.

Iris's eyes cracked faintly open. "Cap?" Her voice sounded rusty, as if left too long in the weather.

"It's Dixie, Grandma." She pulled the thin blanket higher around the knobs that were shoulders and collarbone. "I'm here, Grandma." How had she gotten so old so fast?

Iris's lids creaked up halfway but the gray was cold as if blind. "Ed?"

There was no focus at all in the gaze, and Dix felt a quick splash of ice at her nape and shivered.

"Them boys ... you was with them boys, Ed." Iris frowned in her sleep.

As Dix watched, the eyes seemed to get glassier. "Yer daddy'll switch you, good, when he gets home ... I'm awful ... disappointed ... you." Her voice faded to silence.

Dix smoothed her brow. So many stories I've missed, she thought.

"Awful." Iris started again, rolled to her back, and lay stiff. Dix watched the face, lines twitching, brow creased deeply now and her eyes wet. "No. Ed. Not my son. No."

"Grandma." Dix shook her gently. "It's okay, Grandma, it's just a dream." The lashes fluttered. "It's okay, Grandma; I'm here."

Iris blinked quickly several times. "Dream." She licked her lips, then hoisted herself up on her elbows. "Ehew," she sighed. "Just like I was there again."

She shook her head, hair floating silvery around it. "Awful time."

Dix waited. This was the way the stories usually began. She felt as if a blank tape were beginning to record in the back of her brain; she knew the setting, the scenery, would embroider itself into the fabric of Iris's voice even as the story unraveled.

"No."

Dix jolted out of the warm faraway groove her mind had already settled into.

Iris was shaking her head firmly, looking down at her clasped hands. "No," she said to herself. "Some things are better left unsaid."

Dix felt her mouth open. She felt cheated. "But —"

"No, girl, my storying days are over now." She looked hard at Dix. "Some stories are mine to keep. Some ain't mine to give away, neither." She relaxed back into the pillow and closed her eyes. "Leave me sleep, child."

Dix closed her mouth. Must be a good one, she thought. She rubbed her nose with the feathery pages of her paperback. Shit. She yawned.

"Time for bed, sleepyhead," Betty singsonged in a whisper. Iris groaned with her eyes still closed. "Awake?" Betty mouthed to Dix, who shrugged.

"Good night, Mom." She tried to slip past Betty in the doorway, but her mother followed her out.

"I made your bed with clean sheets, dear." Betty reached out to pat Dix's shoulder but left her hand stranded in the air, undecided.

"You didn't have to do that, Mom." Dix shook her head and turned into the kitchen. "Good night."

Betty followed. "I just ..." She lifted her hands.

Can she say it, Dix wondered.

Betty's eyes shifted around the room, perching briefly on one object after another. "Uh," she faltered again.

"It's okay, Mom," Dix finally sighed.

Let her off the hook again, she thought. "Good night."

The cuckoo recited his line four times, then the little door clicked shut behind him. The big house was silent except for the steady breath of electric fans. Dix stood at the top of the back stairs and followed the long dark gleam of oak flooring down the hall. The brass knob of her own door was cool in her hand. Through the doorway on her right, past the upstairs bath, she could see the small white-sheeted forms of her nephews — the room where they always put the little kids. Mom was staying in Grandma and Cap's room, past hers on the left, still furnished with twin beds, there since Dix could remember. Sarah was in the farthest room on the right. With her door unlocked. Dix held the cool brass in her hand a minute more. It had been a nice Friday night date. Those floorboards looked like they would creak. That front porch kiss. Jasmine. And her door was unlocked.

*T*here is a point of no return. I didn't realize that, really, until I had sex with a woman. There is a place where you cannot go back, cannot do anything but go forward. And you cannot stop.

Elizabethans called orgasm "the little death." I think in many ways they were right, you reach a point in dying, as well as in orgasm, where you cannot stop, cannot go back, can only go forward to meet it. I think that is why Grandma chose to come home to this room, to forgo the chemotherapy that summer, to die.

Perhaps it was that summer that I really began to understand that each instant, each point, is also a point of no return. That life is a series of points with no return. No stops. No going back. Forward motion. And yet, I am back at the Point again.

Saturday Looney Tunes

"Tee hee hee," snickered Wile E. Coyote from the huge console set. Betty stood in the door of Iris's room and shook her head. Melissa ought not let that child watch so much TV. Not healthy.

"Tee hee hee," Red snickered, two feet from the screen, haloed in blue.

"Mornin', sunshine," she said.

Red jerked his head around. "Gramma!" He jerked his head back to the screen at the Road Runner's *Bee beep*. "Bee beep!" he echoed.

"Don't you want to get up and get dressed?"

Red shook his head vigorously without turning.

"I think you ought to turn off that old TV and come help Gramma cook breakfast."

"Uh, uh." Red's eyes didn't move from the screen. "Mommy always lets me watch *Looney Tunes*." He tilted his head back. "It's Saturday, Gramma," he explained.

Betty shook her head. Letting the TV do your babysitting couldn't be good for the children, but Melissa was doing the best she could, she supposed. Three little ones were a handful, and another on the way. Betty smiled, anticipating a new baby in her arms. Babies were the best; they needed everything, and everything they needed was simple to give. "That TV's gonna fry your brain cells," she told Red.

"Granpa watches TV all the time," Red said to the screen.

Betty shook her head and went on through to the kitchen. Kids shouldn't back-talk like that either. Still, Melissa was probably doing the best she could . . . and another baby soon.

The cardinals were at the bird feeder. The coffee made and the grits started, Betty stood at the tall window, hugging herself in the warm morning, watching the birds. The cardinals were her favorites; the gaudy scarlet male with his fierce "pip, pip," the drab but beautiful-in-her-own-subdued-way wife, gently selecting seeds, always vigilant for danger. The male was a flinger. He raked his beak through the trough, and the seeds sprayed out and to the ground where the smaller, plainer birds gleaned among blades of grass. Why was his every motion one of anger?

For her first two weeks here with Iris and Dixie,

Betty had puzzled over the reddish-brown flecks on the side mirror on her car. Blood? Then Dixie had seen the cardinal, had brought Betty onto the back stoop and pointed, and the cardinal had not even noticed them, so intent was he on attacking his reflection. He banged his beak again and again, slipping, then fluttering back to regain his perch to attack again. The female, she supposed, was off doing something constructive, nest-building or eating. Betty only watched for a second, then rushed the car, chased the bird away. She remembered her index finger stretching out in slow motion to touch the red spots on the mirror, staring at the blood spreading into the ridges of her fingerprint.

Now she kept an old sock in the car. When she came back from the market or church or her weekly visit home to pick up the newspapers from the floor, wash Ed's dishes and do his laundry, Betty would carefully wrap the mirror. Somebody had to protect the silly bird from his most stubborn rival.

But he was lovely, she thought, sipping coffee. So bright in the early sun.

"Kin I have some Lucky Charms?" Red tugged at the hem of her nightgown.

"Ooh, you don't want that yucky stuff." Betty shook her head. Melissa really shouldn't feed the kids all that sugar. "How about some yummy bacon and eggs?"

Red screwed up his face. "Uhnt uh. I don't like that runny yellow stuff." He whined, "I want Lucky Charms, Gramma." Betty sighed. He had been so much easier when he was a baby. "Puleese," Red begged.

"Gramma will be sad if you don't eat the breakfast she's been working so hard to make."

Red's face tugged in different directions and a little whimper escaped. Betty's heart twinged. "How about I give you just a handful of Lucky Charms now, and then you try to eat Gramma's breakfast, okay? And I'll scramble up your eggs."

Red grinned and nodded his head fast. He cupped his hands for Betty to fill, and she saw a tell-tale sugary gleam on them. "Did you already have some Lucky Charms?" she asked.

Red's eyes traveled forlornly from his empty hands to her eyes. Silence. Then, "Just the marsh-mallows."

He sounded like a baby and looked so sad, Betty couldn't help but smile. She straightened her face and doled out a bit of the cereal. What a con man.

Betty stared at the grease spreading out from the bacon into the paper towel. She gripped the spatula tighter, tapped the eggs in the carton with her fingernail. Iris was waiting for her breakfast; she'd get cranky pretty soon. Somebody needed to see if Sarah was up yet. Dixie would be asleep until noon after sitting up all night.

"Red!" Her voice came out loud and hard, a surprise. Red's eyes were wide, and he shied back from the door. "Red," Betty consciously softened. "Do Gramma a big favor, okay?" Red nodded cautiously. Betty forced a smile and a note of play into her voice. "Can you be very quiet, like a spy..." She faltered, "like a mouse?" He nodded solemnly. "I want you to go upstairs very quiet and see if Miss Sarah is awake, okay?"

Red began to bounce. "Like a spy on a mission!" he shouted.

Betty pushed down on his shoulders. "Very quiet," she said. "Can you do that?"

He bounced under her hands. "Uh huh, uh huh."

"Yes ma'am," Betty corrected.

"Yes, ma'am," he echoed, still bouncing.

Too much sugar. "Red, I don't want you to wake up anybody else, okay? Aunt Dixie is still asleep, and you have to be very quiet. Okay?"

"Uh huh," he said.

"Yes ma'am."

"Yes ma'am."

"Secret mission," Red whispered. "Spy guy." He sidled off around the doorway into the back stairs. Betty rolled the egg in her palm, then cracked it hard on the frying pan. Dixie promised, she thought. She shook her head sharply, then tried to lose herself in frying eggs.

With Iris served, Betty stood in the window, watching the birds, trying not to listen for sounds upstairs. What was taking Red so long? A lone mockingbird, off from the rest, tugged a worm up from the earth. He . . . she — it was nearly impossible to tell with mockingbirds — seemed to like the company of the birds at the feeder, even though seeds held no interest. Mockingbirds were independent, Betty had noticed, ordinary-looking at first in gray and white, but striking in their mask and sleek larger size. The song was the real beauty of the mockingbird, though, an original jumble of all the other birds' songs, and Betty loved waking in the middle of a spring night to that medley. Iris always said it was the true sign of the end of winter when the mockingbirds sang at night.

What was keeping Red? She walked over and cocked an ear up the stairwell. Voices. Giggles. She started up the steps slowly. Maybe Red was playing with the dog. Maybe she didn't need to go up. A step squeaked suddenly loud, and Betty's heart paused an extra second.

I'm being silly, she thought. Dixie wouldn't lie to me. She's asleep in this room right here at the top of the stairs, and Red's in there playing with the dog. Probably even forgot why I sent him. She paused at the top and looked down the hallway toward Sarah's open doorway. A loud "woof." More giggles.

"Hey, leave me out of this!" Dixie's voice.

Betty stopped in the middle of the hall. I'll just turn and sneak back downstairs, she thought, hunching unconsciously. I don't need to know.

"Oh."

She looked up at the tone in Dixie's voice and saw that she'd seen her. Too late. She drew her shoulders back, felt her mouth draw into the wrinkles Ed so detested, and stepped into the doorway. They all sat up.

"Um, good morning, Mrs. M.," Sarah said and smiled.

Betty quickly dropped her eyes. Their shoulders were awfully naked. "How could you?" she mumbled. Betty felt tears in her throat. How could Dixie do this? "I believed you. You promised." Why was Dixie hurting her like this?

"I'm sorry, Gramma." Red appeared under Betty's downcast eyes. "Don't cry, Gramma."

"I know I wasn't as good a mother as I should have been," Betty began.

"I'll be a good boy, Gramma. Don't cry." Red was near tears himself now. "Don't be sad. I'm sorry. I'll be good."

Sheets rustled and then Dixie was there, wrapped in one. And nothing else. Betty felt her face heat suddenly. "Have you no shame? Why are you doing this to me?" She looked up suddenly, into her daughter's eyes. She really wanted to know. Dixie was tall, a Greek statue reaching out to hug, and Betty felt her body lean toward her.

But Dixie knelt suddenly, and it was Red folding into her arms. "It's not your fault," Dixie whispered, and Red suddenly sobbed. "Gramma's just feeling mad because she isn't happy inside. You *are* a good boy." Betty watched her daughter's hand rubbing circles in the small of Red's back. "Nobody can make Gramma feel better except Gramma, okay?" Red sniffled a little bit, then took the hand Sarah, suddenly dressed in shorts and standing there, offered.

"How dare you," Dixie hissed as soon as they were past the door. "Are you so selfish that you can't see how much that little guy wants to make you happy?"

Betty inhaled sharply. "Selfish! I've done everything I could to make life easier for all of you. And this —" She brushed the sheet. "This is how you thank me." Betty suddenly felt a pang. She sank onto the edge of the bed. "God is punishing me," she murmured.

It was true. She felt it. She had promised to be a missionary when she was fifteen, promised God, and then Ed had come along, and then the babies, and now . . . "God," she began again.

"Don't even start with that promise to God thing, Mom. I've heard it before, and I know better."

Dixie's voice got suddenly soft, and Betty felt the thin fingers on her chin. "Mom." Dixie pushed up, and Betty was forced to meet her gaze. "Mom the only person who's punishing you is you."

Betty caught her breath. "Why are you doing this to me, Dixie?" A tear slid into her mouth, and she spluttered. "I did the best I could." Why couldn't she just leave her alone? Why was she doing this? "Why don't you just let me forget about . . ." Another tear slipped down her neck. She couldn't say it.

Dixie shook her head slowly and blinked hard. "Mom, I'm not doing anything to you. I'm just me. I won't let you —"

"Maybe you and your daddy didn't have such a good relationship, maybe he should have been nicer to you, but —"

"Granny!" Betty and Dixie both swiveled to the sound of Red's voice on the stairs. "You ain't supposed to be up here either. I thought your stair-climber legs was supposed to be busted."

"Mother!" Betty was already at the door. Iris could fall. Had she heard? "Mother, what are you doing up here?"

"I ain't totally dead yet." Iris stood on the landing, breathing hard. "What's the ruckus up there?"

109

"Gramma's feeling mad inside, so me and Zorro's going to eat some Lucky Charms," Red said.

"Let's get you back to bed, Mother." Betty took the older woman's arm, but she didn't budge.

"What's going on," Iris demanded.

Dixie came down and took the other arm. "Nothing Grandma," she said.

Iris looked from one to the other, then shook her head. "Nothing worse than bein' so old you get left out of everything," she muttered. "Might as well be dead, I reckon."

Betty grabbed her mother-in-law's arm again. "Come on, now."

Iris gave her that same look she'd given her the day Ed had brought her home the first time. Nobody appreciated anything, it seemed. Least of all Iris. But then, what did she really expect? The woman was dying. No mother liked the woman who took her son away... Well, she herself did like Melissa... "Come on now," she said.

"Yeah, Granny, you can have Lucky Charms and watch *Looney Tunes* with me if you want," Red said. "That's better than bein' dead, ain't it?"

Iris snorted, turning carefully on the stairs. "Reckon I don't have to turn on the TV to watch *Looney Tunes* in this house," she muttered.

*I*t's not polite to point," Mom always said. But oh, how she wanted to. Who could she blame? Whom could she point at? Who was it safe to blame? Only herself really.

We sat at the kitchen table, watching the birds at the bird feeder, and I listened to her trying to find a direction in which to point. "Your daddy was hard on you," she said. "I know that girls who don't have a good relationship with their father are more likely to be . . . you know . . ." She sighed and looked at her fingers wrapped tight around her iced tea glass. "But *he was doing the best he could ... Iris was hard on him, I think ... but she had all those children and her sisters' children too to look after, and she married young, but they all did back then, and ..."*

She looked away from me at the birds and frowned. I could almost hear the whisperings in her mind, faster and faster.

"I don't think it's natural, Dixie," she said firmly. "God might put those temptations before us, but it is because we are fallen. We were cast out of the garden. We must overcome the temptations, and we can, I know we can, with the help of the Lord."

"Is it my fault then, Mom? Do you blame me? Do you hate me for being the sinner?"

I know the route those whispers in my mother's head follow because I have followed them myself. I did not love him enough, I did not love her enough, I am unhappy because there is something wrong with me, he she they are unhappy because I am doing have done am thinking have thought have been will be, am, bad.

"No, Mom. I am not."

"We must hate the sin and love the sinner." She stared and blinked at the window, and we both knew the route she was following, and the circling back to the place she always began. "We all have a cross to bear. Ed is right; it is the mother's task to raise her children up in the ways of righteousness."

All of those fingers pointing at my mother, all of them her own.

Shelling Peas and Q's

"I Swanee! Like my sister Rosie used to say, 'The old devil's lettin' some steam out of the oven today.'" Iris sprawled her legs wide as the lawn chair would allow and fanned down the front of her house dress. "Don't you go pointin' that thing at me, girlie." She snapped her fan shut and waggled it at Sarah, who laughed behind her camera. "I ain't dignified today."

Sarah snapped anyway. "If you're not dignified, Iris, I don't know what dignified is," she said.

These would be great shots, she thought. The pecan tree they sat under filtered the mid-morning

113

sun, and the faded pink of Iris's thin dress seemed soft and childlike on the old woman's ramshackle form. Her face was really quite beautiful, tired and lined, but her skin was powdery and nearly translucent.

Iris grinned and the painful furrow between her brows flattened out; shadows rippled into ancient eddies of lines at the corners of her mouth and eyes. Sarah thought of the faint map a smile drew on Dix's face; would she see it fully etched someday? Would she be there to watch time sharpen the contrast?

The back door slammed and Betty appeared with a pitcher of iced tea and four clinking glasses. Sarah zoomed in on her face, her shoulders, her arms, pale brown freckles, a scowl of concentration, tea splashing from the pitcher in her right hand, and the clenched-tight fingers, one to a glass, of her left. Or was that scowl for Sarah? Or for Dix? Through the camera lens, Sarah saw the dark circles from those earlier tears. Sarah snapped, wondering, is this what a mother is supposed to be?

She knew her own picture of "mother" — and "family" as well, she supposed — was a bit blurry. Mama was a thin redhead in a blue dress, framed in tarnished brass, carefully packed and unpacked, placed on a dresser or shelf in one foster home after another. The women there were Mrs. This or That, occasionally kind, usually harried with trying to keep things — their marriages, their homes, their own families — together. Sarah had learned early on that no matter how good she was, how hard she tried, she was optional. Things got bad, she was the one to go, starting with Mama.

Betty carefully pouring the tea now, was no different, Sarah figured. Dix had been a pretty good kid, thirty years' worth, up until now. Soon as she stopped fitting into her folks' neat little picture, they'd just crop her out. At least that was the way it seemed to work as far as Sarah could see.

Still, it would be nice to have the history. Listening to Iris and Dix — ("You remember my sister, Rose, she . . ." and "Now your mother came from upriver where Cap used to take me fishing . . .") — Sarah felt woven into some intricate mesh, like the branches of the pecan tree overhead. She felt part of it, a leaf out there on the end of some branch, fluttering in every strong gust, though her hold on Dix's branch was a bit tenuous. Much as she didn't want to hang on, being even a little bit connected to those stories felt good. She had to admit it, that was part of what she wanted from Dix. Family. Something to be connected to . . . someone. First time for everything, she thought.

"So, where do your people come from?" Iris asked. "Don't believe I reckonize any partic'lar accent in ya." She cracked a smile. "Ya don't hail from these parts, that's for sure."

"Dix doesn't have an accent, and she's from here," Sarah responded, thinking fast.

"Oh, that's what happens to the youngsters . . . 'shamed of the South 'n all. Think a drawl sounds uneducated. Teach 'em that in them Yankee colleges, so the young'uns try to citify. That what happened to you?" Iris wasn't going to let her off the hook. "Your folks send you to some cold place where they ain't no music to the words?"

Sarah looked to Betty, who was intent on pouring

115

tea into tall glasses. No rescue there; still mad, Sarah guessed. They had talked a long time when Betty had come down to St. Pete to visit. Betty had been super-sympathetic; lots of her elementary kids were in the same situation Sarah had been in. Iris waited, hands folded. "I haven't got any folks," Sarah finally said. "None that matter anyway."

Iris snorted. "Everybody's got folks, whether they're kin or not . . . and they all matter, don't fool yourself on that one, girl." She squinted across at Sarah, who saw her through the camera lens. "And don't go pointin' that thing at me. Look me eye to eye and tell me you don't got no folks that matter."

Sarah flushed warm, and rested the heavy camera in her lap. She felt a trickle of sweat stream down the nape of her neck under her ponytail. What the hell was taking Dix so long with those peas?

"Well?" Iris said. Betty's stare was fixed on the bird feeder off to the side of the house. Sarah looked down and wiggled the film advance lever on her camera.

"I don't know who my father is, and they took me away from my mother when I was five," she said. She looked up into Iris's gaze. "No folks. No one that matters."

Iris didn't blink. Dix and Red's laughter spilled into the silence from the direction of the garden. Iris nodded her head to that side, and, still holding Sarah's eyes, asked, "What about that one?"

"Oh here comes Dixie and Red with the peas," Betty spluttered, jumped up, and grabbed Sarah's arm. "They probably want some help."

Sarah twisted back to keep Iris's gaze as Betty dragged her off; what did that look mean?

Iris closed her eyes and leaned back in the lawn chair, legs still sprawled, hands clasped in her lap. There was something awfully smug in that expression, Sarah thought.

As soon as they met the two dragging buckets from the garden, Sarah loosed herself from Betty and took a grip of her own on Dix's arm. "I think your grandmother knows," she said.

Dix frowned and squinted, then her eyes opened wide.

"Knows what?" Red demanded.

"Why?" Dix asked. "What happened?" Sarah felt the tension in her forearm; Dix was nearly trembling.

"Nothing," Betty said firmly.

"Knows what?" Red repeated.

"Nothing." Betty glared at Sarah and Dix.

They all stood staring at each other in the direct sun for a long few minutes. It got hotter and stiller. A mockingbird started up suddenly in the high branches of the pecan tree. "Nothing to know," Betty finally said. "Nothing to say."

"Better stop dillydallying around over there," Iris called. "Got to get them peas shelled and snapped and on the stove before eleven if we want 'em for dinner today."

"It's okay," Sarah said to Dix, dropping her arm. "Later."

Sarah moved around the edge of the circle of lawn chairs, kneeling to shoot close-ups of hands just as a hull snapped or a thin finger scooted peas from the shell. She caught Betty's buck-toothed grin and

Red untying his great-grandmother's shoe. She captured Dix's green eyes shadowed by dark lashes.

She paused, toes curling into the wide, cool blades of grass. That's how she had first seen Dix, looking down, quiet and removed behind those lashes.

The English department office had been chaotic, kids jostling and shouting behind Sarah, a mimeograph machine clunking away in the corner, two teachers arguing beside Dix's desk, one loading books on a cart, two others joshing at the coffee maker. When she had seen Dix sitting there, an island of serenity in the midst of voices and bells and all that high school drama, Sarah knew this was the woman she had spoken to on the phone. She also knew this was a woman she wanted to know.

Iris seemed to read her mind. "I done said ta stop pointin' that dad-blamed camera at me," she said. "Pull you up a chair and be sociable." Iris reached back and dragged another lawn chair into the circle. "Give this girl a mess of them peas so she kin earn her supper."

Sarah sat down and took a handful of green like the others, pushed the first hull to pop it open, and slid her thumb through the shell to push the peas into the wash pan on her lap. They thwopped hollowly, and the sound was echoed around the circle.

"Now how 'zackly did you and Dixie come to be friends?" Iris asked.

Sarah hesitated and looked up to see Dix staring back a little wide-eyed. Play it straight, she thought.

"Well," she began, "I covered that story about her class teaching the little kids at the elementary school . . . You know, when they wrote children's books. You have it on your refrigerator."

Iris nodded. "Yep, that's a right nice picture, too." Her eyes narrowed, her hands working automatically. "Reckon you two had a lot in common?"

Sarah looked back down at the bowl of peas. I reckon, she thought. "Yes, ma'am," she said, still watching her fingers, the nails now green, pushing the family of tiny brown peas from their pocket.

Betty finally came to the rescue. "Oh, you know how it is with young people, Mother," she said. "Going to parties, going to the beach, eating in restaurants..."

Sarah concentrated on her hands. How they met... That was one story she had... one she couldn't tell here. Watching each other around the edges of kids. Nothing said except in that silent language of looks. Are you? Aren't you? Why haven't I seen you before? Where can I see you again?

The teenagers in Dix's class had fixed it for them. "Grading papers at the beach this weekend, Ms. M.?" that grinning jock had asked. "With plenty of volleyball breaks," another chimed in, and she had grinned and nodded and looked my way.

"Yeah, you'll probably find a little sand in those essays on Monday," Dix had said. "Just don't let me see your faces at Pass-a-Grille or the grit might rub off on your grades." In code, direct to me, Pass-a-Grille, the gay beach, The Tree, the women's bar. I knew she would be looking for my face there.

Maybe that would be our family story someday, Sarah thought. Maybe she and Dix could build from that story.

A bean hit her square between the eyes. "Hey!" Sarah looked up.

Dix's freckles squinched into the lines of her grin.

"Wake up over there. I'm supposed to be the sleepy one," Dix said.

Sarah didn't even think. She stuck out her tongue in her usual response. "And who do you think kept you —"

Sarah caught her tongue between her teeth as Dix blushed. The dark lashes fell. Betty cleared her throat. Ooops. She felt a rush of blood to her own ears. The mockingbird chuckled a short burst in the treetop. A few minutes passed with no sound but the snap and thwonk of peas into buckets and dishpans.

"Young folks," Iris snorted finally. "Don't reckon I do know much 'bout how it is with 'em these days," she said, returning to Betty's theme. She turned to Sarah. "You all drink hard liquor out there?" she asked. "The only thing we used to go to the beach for was to dig up turtle eggs and cast net for mullet. Maybe take a picnic, let the children build sand castles. Never much liked it myself . . . not a speck of shade, and sticky, and all that sand to get tracked into the house. Just what do you do out there?"

"Well," Sarah started slow, thinking fast. "There's the sun. Most people want a tan these days . . ."

"Just askin' for skin cancer," Betty mumbled. "Do you wear sun screen, Dixie?" She turned to her daughter and began to lecture on Uncle Jerome who had had large portions of his face removed due to melanoma.

"And there's usually a volleyball game or football or something," said Sarah. "Everybody pretty much knows everybody at the beach we go to, so I suppose you could say it's like a big picnic." She tried to give Iris an acceptable version of the green-gulf, white-sand scene of bikinis and oily tattooed skin and beers in coolers... "The sunsets are gorgeous on the Gulf you know." ...and boys cruising boys and girls cruising girls and couples wandering off into the dunes. "There's one, uh, dance club on the beach where you can dance, and another place where you can sit outside and listen to a singer and talk to your friends." Or kiss quietly in a corner under palm fronds and stars, like that first time with Dix.

"Talk, eh?" Iris looked skeptical. " 'Magine there's a bit of drinkin' goes on them places too?"

"Some," Sarah nodded. Dix's kiss had tasted of blackberry seltzer that night; neither of them were big drinkers.

"Well, my 'sperience is that where there's young'uns and liquor, there's bound ta be a ruckus," Iris said.

"I don't know if Dix and I are exactly young'uns," Sarah stuck in, but Iris had a story rolling now and didn't pause.

"You take Dixie's daddy, now," she said. "The onliest time I ever knowed him to touch a drop was when he was 'bout seventeen, and Lord, the ruckus that that boy got himself into."

Iris settled back into her lawn chair with some rusty squeaks. Sarah glanced at Dix, who was frowning at her mother and shaking her head, answering softly. The dry touch of Iris's finger brought her back to their own conversation. "Ed never has been mucha one for talkin', but I heard all about it from Miz Kuttle. I was visitin' with her this one particular evenin', went over there to take her collards, I think, an' she started goin' on 'bout how she thought it was a fine thing her boys was doin', they'd started some club called the Crusaders to keep

121

'that element' out. 'Gotta let 'em know we're a Christian community here,' she said. Well, I Swanee, I didn't have the vaguest notion what that woman was goin' on about, but her bein' the preacher's wife 'n all, I just smiled and nodded and tried ta figure things out, careful-like. So finally she says somethin' 'bout Ed, an' my ears prick up. 'Don't know why that boy 'a yours ain't more involved with the Crusaders,' she says, so I run right home 'n grab Ed by the ear 'n tell him to get his heart right with the Lord and get involved in this here club the Kuttle boys got goin'. Suppose I shoulda got my ducks in a row before I done that, but it all turned out for the best, I reckon."

Iris stopped and stared off toward the garden for a long minute. "Yep, reckon if more people'd done what those boys done, we'd not be havin' the worries we got in this old world today."

Sarah felt her brow crease. What the hell was Iris getting to? She looked over at Dix, who gave her a quick, quizzical glance, then refocused on whatever Betty was saying.

"Must be the last days for sure," Iris muttered.

Ah, Sarah thought, the religious stuff. This fundamentalist strain was pretty wild, but she figured not many people really bought into it these days. Dix had always made it sound like her folks were fanatics, but nobody could really be that out of touch. The mockingbird in the high branches chortled lazily.

"Reckon Ed needed more than just his mama's push," Iris chuckled. "When he come home that night, he reeked of corn squeezin's. 'Course Cap whupped him good for drinkin', but we was all glad they run that fella off like they done."

When Sarah looked up into the silence, she found Iris's eyes riveted on her, the gray as dark and hard as the blade of a new shovel. Her own hands stopped, the pea pod pregnant with lumps between her fingers.

"One 'a *them*," Iris said dramatically.

Sarah looked over at Dix. Was Iris saying what she thought she was saying? Both Dix and Betty stared back, mouths slightly dropped. She looked back at Iris. "What?" she said.

"One 'a *them*," Iris repeated. "You know, funny." Her thinning eyebrows lifted.

Sarah let her face go blank, her forehead smooth. "What do you mean?" Everything seemed to have fallen silent: mockingbird, cicadas, green rustlings in the treetop.

Iris rolled her eyes. She lowered her voice. "Teacher at the high school," she said. "Yankee." She nodded slightly, as if that explained it.

Sarah could see the hairs of her eyebrows, they were wrinkled so low. She waited.

"One 'a the Kuttle boys told his mama that fella touched him . . . you know, tried to hug him." Iris bent closer. "We all thought he was kinda funny from the first, wearin' them floweredy shirts, and he had this real purty, kinda pale, thin skin. Kinda bluish." She paused again. "Like a girl's, if you know what I mean."

"Shit." It just came out. Even she heard the note of wonder in her voice. How could anyone still think like this?

Dix inhaled sharply.

"Oh, sorry," Sarah said, "Um, excuse me, I just —"

Iris's brows were low now, and she bent in toward Sarah suddenly. "Ever see somebody tarred and feathered, Missy?"

Sarah drew back. "Wha —"

"That's what them Kuttle boys 'n my Ed did ta that fella. Poured hot tar on 'im, dumped a croaker sack 'a feathers over 'im, and dumped 'im outside 'a town."

Sarah could taste the older woman's breath, she was so close, humid and tea-soured.

"Don't tell me liquor never led to nothin' evil," she hissed.

Sarah tried to catch her breath in the heat, but her lungs felt heavy and full. Which was the evil, she wondered. "Who are you calling evil, Mrs. Major?" she said, low and breathless.

"Sign of the last days," Betty said.

"Shoo," Iris cut in, "Sign 'a last days . . . more just pure sign 'a got too much 'n not enough to do. Breakdown of the family, breakdown of everything. Been happenin' long 's I been around. Ain't goin' ta stop. Young'uns are goin' ta be young and foolish always. The devil's bound ta have his way, long as they ain't got no family ta' keep 'em tied down and busy."

"Now wait a minute, Grandma." Sarah saw Dix grin to show she wasn't being rude. "I'm not so young, and everybody knows teachers haven't 'got too much,' and I'm hardly the breakdown of society."

"And it sounds to me like it was his 'family' that got him into trouble," Sarah said.

Dix frowned at her. "He was young," she said.

"Defending him, eh?" Sarah wanted to take the words back as soon as they came out.

124

Dix's eyes flew wide and she opened her mouth. "Who asked —"

Betty grabbed her daughter's arm. "Shhh. Don't —"

Her heart jerked toward Dix, the green eyes hard and her forehead creased. "Sorry," she stuttered, and Dix looked down at the long thin fingers of her mother's hand on her arm.

Sarah glanced back at Iris. The old woman's lips were tight, and she concentrated on the peas she sifted through her fingers. Betty glared at Sarah. Dix didn't look up.

"Maybe I don't belong here," Sarah said. She heard a seven-year-old voice in her head repeating, fucking family fucking family who needs 'em who needs 'em. Fumbling underneath her lawn chair, she found the camera strap. Got to get out of here, she thought, and stood up.

"Now," Iris said. "Now, hold on, Missy." She stomped her foot down on the strap. "You don't strike me as the type to give in so easy."

Sarah stood, her hand sweaty on the leather strap, feeling trapped.

Iris leaned forward over her dishpan. "Maybe the heat's just got to you." Her eyes held Sarah's and her voice held the tone of command. "Sit down and shell that mess of peas."

"Stay, Sarah." Dix's voice was soothing, and it seemed to come from far off.

Sarah tilted her head to look. Dix's eyes were the same calm she had seen in that school office that first time, back in October . . . hurricane season. So maybe she didn't have to weather any more storms alone. Sarah knew she didn't want to. She sat down.

"Have you heard anything from those colleges yet, Dixie?" Smooth, Betty, Sarah thought.

"Well, you know I've been accepted by all three, Mom," Dix said. "Nothing yet on money." She rolled her head back to loosen her neck and remained looking up into the tree. "Who knows."

"Now 'zackly where are these schools?" Iris said. "You ain't thinkin' 'bout goin' back up north again are ya?"

"You know I am, Grandma," Dix said softly. "We talked about this last week."

Iris shook her head. "Unnatural," she muttered. "Can't understand why you'd want ta go and break you mama's heart like that for —"

"I want my daughter to be happy, that's all," Betty said, and stopped, looking as surprised as everyone else at the solid tone of her voice. "Well, I do," she said, and nodded sharply to herself, looking down at the hulls sifting through her fingers. "Whether Dixie wants to go to Colorado or New York or stay down in Gainesville, she should."

"Land sakes, woman," Iris spluttered. "You need that girl here, and she oughta know that family means more than any college degree. Already got one anyhow."

"Now wait a minute, Grandma," Dix said.

"With all respect, Mother," Betty said, "family is not something you cut off like a foot in a trap and leave behind."

Sarah felt like a spectator at a tennis match. Her head snapped back and forth. She realized her mouth was open and she consciously closed it. A family never talked like this.

"Maybe I'm going to take family with me," Dix said.

The silence was immediate. Sarah's eyes snapped to Dix. She felt her jaw hanging again and closed it.

"Um," Dix looked down. "Never mind," she mumbled.

Iris glanced appraisingly from Dix to Sarah to Dix to Betty. "Hmmm," she said. "Shore is hot today, eh?" She popped a bean loudly. They all concentrated on their hands for a long few minutes until the mockingbird started up again.

"Wonder what those boys've got themselves into?" Betty said halfheartedly. She scanned the yard, and Sarah knew she was seeing the trees a little boy could fall from, the gardening shed with sharp tools and poisons, the garage with dangling wires and flammables.

"He's fine, Mom," Dix said. She shook her head tiredly. "Stop worrying so much. Let him be a kid."

Betty smiled at her daughter, her brow clear and nose mottled with freckles and shadow through the leaves. Sarah wished her camera were in her hands for that shot.

"Never had to worry about you, did I?" Betty shook her head, still smiling, her teeth slightly bucked, unconsciously lovely. "You always took care of yourself, always entertained yourself . . . didn't need anything but a book."

Sarah watched her lover's eyes, downcast, shadowed. They had talked about this early on in their relationship . . . yelled about it actually. Things had begun to get serious, three months together and they had agreed to be monogamous. But there were still separate lives, engagements, and no "real commitment"; they were together maybe a couple of nights a week, then, out of the blue, Dix says, "It's over, you don't have time for me" just because she had gone out with an old friend one of "their" nights. Sarah hadn't let her run away though, she'd confronted her, made Dix yell back, held her until the back-story came out, till the tears.

"Sounds kind of lonely for a little girl," Sarah said softly now. Maybe it was time for Dix to meet this one head-on.

She glanced up to see Dix's green gaze, calm and a little creased at the edges. Scared. She had gotten the message.

"Oh, Dixie was always just fine," Betty said. "She was such a good girl, no worry at all." Her voice was light and sure, nearly the same tone as the cardinal piping in the holly tree. Sarah caught a glimpse of Red's blue shirt by the goldfish pool at the bottom of the yard.

"Just fine," Iris murmured with a note of question almost disappearing at the end. "You did like your books, Dixie," she said, and hunched forward. "I remember sittin' here, snappin' peas just like this, an' you rattlin' on an' on 'bout some book." Dix's gaze met Iris's across the circle of green lawn, and Sarah felt her own smile spread to her ears.

"Rattlin' on?" Betty looked puzzled. "Why Dixie, you never did say much more'n a word to me 'bout anything you were reading. I'd ask what you were reading and you'd say 'Nothing, Mom.'" Betty's voice held a note of hurt. "You were always such a private child," she explained to herself.

"Maybe you didn't hear me, Mom," Dix said gently.

Betty looked over, and her hands ceased moving suddenly. "What do you mean, Dixie?" Betty looked frightened, Sarah thought. "I don't know what you mean."

Dix reached over and wrapped slender fingers around her mother's wrist. "Maybe you didn't hear me," she repeated. She blinked and looked off into the garden. "Maybe I didn't speak loudly enough," she said, as if to herself.

"I always tried to be there for you," Betty protested. "What do you mean? I drove to games and practices and I worked so we could afford uniforms and coaches and . . ."

"That was Buddy, Mom," Dix said. "I didn't do that stuff, Buddy did." She swallowed. "I'm not blaming you, Mom, I'm just sorry I didn't ask for more of your time, more of you."

Betty was crying. "I did the best I could." She sniffed. "I know it's all my fault . . ." She stopped and inhaled suddenly.

They all looked at Iris, who continued to snap calmly. "Seems ta me," she finally said, slowly meeting the eyes of each of the others in turn. "Seems t' me, some young'uns is better seen 'n not heard sometimes." She paused and chewed a pea pod slowly. "P'rhaps it's time we all learnt somethin' 'bout manners."

*S*ince then, since that summer, she has signed her name a slashing Z. It is like a tattoo. A scar. A blade slicing precisely to the point. Sarah. My Zorro.

She came here that summer and showed me things I had not seen before in the things I had always seen. She turned my body and held my head and made me look into the face of things. A new lens. She pointed me in a different direction which was the same direction; she pointed it out.

And how could I not rock back into the arms that

held me so firmly? Into soft breasts, solid thighs, warm breath of wisteria and jasmine, the song of the mockingbird?

I slept in the upstairs east bedroom last night, and I felt her arms around me, holding my gaze in the right direction. Her letter is beside her photo on my desk, and I cannot help listening for the crunch of her truck tires on the gravel drive. The slash of her Z on her letter. The slash of the Z on the truck. The mark on me.

A Picnic
Is Not Always Easy

Ed downshifted, gears grinding just a little at first, ignoring Bud's grimace, and eased her off the highway onto Mama's street.

"Watch the oa —" Bud clamped his jaw down.

Shoot, Ed thought, so he'd broken a little branch and there was a big hunk of moss dangling from the hook, there wasn't nothin' to driving this rig. You'd think he'd never sat behind the wheel of a semi, the way that boy went on about him driving the crane truck. Downright disrespectful sometimes. He gunned the engine a couple of times without thinking. He couldn't figure what he'd done to raise such kids. He saw old Miz Rainey push herself back into the azalea bushes on the left as they passed, and he tipped his Major Construction cap in thanks.

"Maybe you ought to slow down, Dad," Buddy said.

Ed gunned the engine in response. "Cain't give me an ounce a' credit, kin ya, boy?" He spit hard out the window and shook his head. "Get kids of your own an' ya think ya know it all," he muttered.

Buddy, Dixie, even Betty... all against him, he thought. He didn't know why. He'd done his best to give 'em a good home, teach 'em values. "No respect at all," he muttered.

"Give respect, might get it back," Buddy retorted.

Ed snapped his head around. "What's got into you today, boy?"

Bud's cool green eyes met his gaze steadily. "Just think you reap what you sow, Dad. Isn't that what the Good Book says?"

Ed started shoving down on the brake pedal and shifted down. "Gettin' awful big for your britches, aren't ya?" He spat out the window again and shook his head to himself. "First Dixie, now you... Don't know what your mother done..."

"Don't even start in on Mom." Bud pounded his fist once on the dash and when Ed looked over, he had twisted in his seat to face him. Bud's heavy brow was dark. "Whatever's wrong in this family sure isn't her fault. It's the 'sins of the fathers,' remember, Dad?"

Ed couldn't believe it. Bud hadn't back-talked him

since he was a teenager. First Dixie'd gone off to school and been corrupted, and now this. Enough to break his heart. They couldn't see he'd been tough for their own good. "My own son," he muttered.

"Yes, I am your own son," Bud said. "And Dix is your own daughter, too." Bud took an audible breath and let it out slow, then continued more softly. "If there's anything wrong with this family, you're gonna have to think about maybe bein' a part of the reason, Dad."

Ed jumped when Bud touched his arm, first time in years he'd touched him. He mashed the brake pedal harder than he meant to, and they both lurched.

"I don't like it any more than you do, Dad, but Dixie's my sister, and I'm not going to lose her out of my family just because she's weird."

"Sinner," Ed said, disgusted. "Can't give my blessing to that. Unnatural. The devil's work." Mama's drive approached more quickly than it should have, and Ed's thigh ached a bit as he tried to slow the semi.

"It's not for us to judge, Dad . . ."

Ed saw Buddy brace himself against the dash as the truck ate up the quiet, oak-lined street. "And Sarah's not so bad either. For cryin' out loud, Dad, they're just people."

Ed heard a note of hysteria in his son's voice that had nothing to do with Dixie or Sarah. "Slow it down, Dad!"

The truck grumbled on, and Ed grinned over at Bud. "Scared, boy?" He thought about Bud asking to race a stock car when he was a teenager. *He'd* been the one scared then. Of course he'd told him just plain no, not that he was worried he'd lose his boy in a wreck on a dirt track. "Shoot, I been drivin' heavy equipment since before you was thought of. Was drivin' 'em in Korea when I was just sixteen."

He tilted his cap back, one hand on the wheel, and glanced at the road. His thigh ached a little. "They's some say the Communists is 'just people' too, you know. Danged if I'm lettin' any 'a them in my family, either."

She'll change her mind, he thought. All young'uns rebel some. His hands gripped the wheel a little tighter. Slow down, dang it, he thought.

"Dad." Bud was staring ahead, face stiff.

"Lez-beans," he said, and spat out the window. "Pure sinners, that's what I say."

"Dad!" Bud shouted as Ed whipped the big steering wheel nonchalantly and the crane truck slithered along the gravel drive of his mother's house. What the heck? He pumped the brake. They slid on another foot or two before the wheels gripped.

Too late. Dang it. The hook of the crane slapped lazily against the upstairs porch railing and chunks of wood sprayed out.

"Dagnab it!" he muttered, as a two-by-four thonked the hood of his truck, denting it. The semi, finally under control, crawled up the drive slowly. "Must be somethin' wrong with those tires," he said.

"You can't expect any tires to grab onto gravel under this kind of weight at that speed, Dad."

"You think I'm some kinda fool, boy?" Ed realized his hands were slick and cramped on the steering wheel. "Bet you ain't checked those tires in months.

Your job is to check those tires." He shook his head and muttered to himself, "Cain't trust nobody but yerself these days, I reckon."

Bud opened his door and swung out before the truck was stopped. Standing on the runner, he stared angrily into Ed's eyes. "Can't trust somebody who's your family if you can't trust 'em to love you first, I reckon," he said, and slammed the door back.

Ed snorted at Bud's wide back striding away. Love . . . Betty'd messed both them kids up but good. Love was somethin' you outgrew. If you loved somebody, you sacrificed something of yourself, like God did Jesus, and after you died, God paid you back. He'd given up all the adventure and life of bein' a young single fella for this family, and none of 'em appreciated it a bit.

He sat in the cab for a minute, gripping and relaxing his hands, watching Bud walk to the circle of women under the pecan tree. They all smiled and laughed at something he said . . . probably about me, Ed thought.

Bud was a good lookin' man, he supposed. And there he went, like always, a kissin' and a huggin' on his mama and his grandma and his sister. Least he didn't mess none with that Sarah woman.

Ed felt his temple pounding under the band of his hat. Somethin' wrong with that boy he couldn't figure out . . . Betty's fault fer sure. Always babyin' him. Heck, she'd ruined both of 'em. 'Course he'd had to be extra tough with his kids, to make up for her being so nice to 'em. Now anybody could see that. He spat out the window again.

Wham! Something hit hard against the passenger door, and Ed jumped and looked over.

"Granpa!" Red climbed up and scrambled across into Ed's lap, Dixie's big black dog behind him. "Lehme drive, Granpa," Red demanded, shoving against his hip. "Get on outa the way."

Ed couldn't help but grin. Now here was somebody who loved him. This was one boy nobody was gonna push around . . . just like his grandpa. Best thing about grandkids, you didn't have to be tough with 'em, you could just plain love 'em. He ruffled the little guy's mop of hair. "How ya doin' pal?"

"Move it, old man," the little boy said.

Betty would have a fit if she heard Red talkin' like that, but Ed knew this little fella wasn't gonna be nobody's fool, no ladies man, and no queer-boy either. He was smart and tough and Ed couldn't help but hug him before shoving his way out of the door. Red squirmed back and punched him on the arm.

Ed stood on the running step. "Where ya takin' her, sport?"

Red jammed a Major Construction cap down over his ears and hooked an arm around the steering wheel.

Just like Granpa, Ed thought.

"Got a job over to Valdosta," he replied. He sat up on his knees so he could see out. "Now get outa the way, old man, I got to hit the road."

Chip off the old block, Ed thought, swinging himself down, slamming the door behind him. Red pretended to start the truck, roared like the engine, and gave Ed a perfunctory wave, elbow out the window.

The old place looked good, he thought as he strolled across the yard. Must be havin' dinner outside — lawn chairs scattered in an odd circle, the plywood table built around the trunk of the pecan covered in plastic table cloths. Somebody had cut the grass; he could smell the fresh watermelon scent and his work boots scuffed up clippings. He kind of wished he could take off his shoes; his feet remembered how cool and tingly soft fresh-mowed grass felt. One 'a the good things about bein' a kid, he thought. Maybe when Red got through playin' in the truck . . .

"Havin' a hen party here?" Ed said to the group. They sort of chuckled, Dixie scowling as usual, and Bud looked off down the yard. "All that cacklin' and scratchin' 'bout the dust, ya know . . ." Ed tilted his hat back and put his hands in his back pockets. "Y'all manage to cook some dinner in between yer cluckin'? Workin' man needs ta eat, ya know."

"Keep your pants on, son," Iris said. "We been workin' all mornin' too."

She looked like a tiny queen sittin' there in that lawn chair, Ed thought. Now she'd sacrificed all right, and he loved her for it. Her eyes held his for a long minute, then he had to look away.

"If you're so all-fired hungry," she said, "you kin help these womenfolk haul some of that food outa the kitchen."

"No," Betty piped up. "You just set yourself down and I'll go get you some ice tea. You been out in that hot sun all mornin'." But here she was, lookin' at Buddy the whole dang time she was rattling on. "I just bet you didn't drink near enough fluids," she said.

"Just go on an' get me some tea," Ed growled, and lowered himself carefully into a squeaking chair.

Betty and Bud exchanged frowns. Turning toward

the kitchen, he heard her mumbling as she walked away, "Don't come complainin' to me when you get leg cramps all night..." Ed decided not to hear and leaned back and shut his eyes.

"I'll give you a hand, Mama," Bud said and headed toward the back door.

"Don't know why she puts up with it," Dixie mumbled.

I don't hear that either, he thought. Probably talkin' to that Sarah person anyway.

"Honor thy mother and thy father that your days may be long upon the earth," he said to the air, eyes still closed. She'd just better watch out, or the Lord would strike her down. Sometimes he had a real hard time acceptin' the Lord movin' in mysterious ways. A shiver ran down his back. Why didn't she just get herself right with God 'n quit actin' stubborn? He heard his mama's snort.

"Reckon there's somethin' to be said for puttin' up with anything," she said.

Ed opened his eyes to the dancing green leaves of the pecan tree overhead. What the heck was that supposed to mean? He wasn't about to tolerate foolishness from anybody.

"Is it okay for Red to be in that truck by himself?" Sarah asked.

Ed looked over at her, the wind lifting the few strands of her red hair that had worked loose from the ponytail. She sure did remind him of Betty when she was a young woman. He always had been a sucker for redheads.

"Can't do a bit of harm," he said to her. "Can't reach the pedals. No keys."

He caught a glimpse of Dixie leaning forward

139

from her seat on the board swing, staring at Sarah, a
sweet smile curving the left corner of her mouth. He
always used to catch her smiling like that at him
when she was a little tyke. His voice caught as he
continued, "Good for kids to play at being grownups."

Dixie glanced hard at him when she saw him
looking at her, then down at the bare spot of earth
below the swing. She'd always been the good one,
independent, for a girl. Real quiet. Made up games
for herself, just like Red was doin' now.

"He ain't no bother to nobody when he's playin'
like that," Ed said. It came out softer than he
usually talked, so he gruffed his voice down. "Let 'im
learn how to take care of himself."

Sarah laughed. "Long as there's no keys," she
said and shook her head. She picked up the camera
and fiddled with something. "I can just see him
driving right through the picnic, you know."

Her long legs stretched out ahead as she moved
across the shadowed lawn toward Red. Quite a looker,
Ed thought. "Some kind of babysitter," he heard her
mutter.

Iris snorted. "I like this girl," she said.

Dixie looked up and smiled at her grandmother.

Iris said, "Always say, you can judge a person by
the friends they choose, and I'd say you choose 'em
pretty good, girl."

Dixie nodded. "She is nice."

Ed felt his chest constrict. Mama didn't know
what she was sayin', he reminded himself and
controlled the growl welling up.

"I'd hate to lose her," Dixie murmured. She

kicked the swing back a little and pressed her face against the rope.

"So don't," Iris said. "Friends is to keep."

Ed looked over at his mother. Stay out of it, old woman, he thought. If Dixie could get away from that woman, maybe she'd see the light. She was just all cloudy with this "love" foolishness. He was itchin' to say somethin'. Dang Dixie for bein' so stubborn.

"If I go away to school . . ." Dixie shrugged.

Iris looked at Dixie speculatively. "Reckon she said somethin' to me 'bout maybe movin' on up north herself," she said.

Ed's jaw wanted to drop, but he clenched hard. Mama don't know nothin', he told himself. He looked over to see Dixie scuff to a sudden stop in the swing.

"Said somethin' 'bout havin' job offers in Colorado and Yankee-land too," Iris continued.

Dixie's mouth opened and closed quickly. "Um," she said. She looked quickly back toward the truck where Sarah stood on the bumper, snapping away at Red. "She said that?" she asked.

Hmmm, Ed thought, more than meets the eye here. Better try to get the lay of the land from Betty. Dang it, if only he could just ask Dixie straight out.

The back door squeaked open, and Betty leaned out. "Think I can get some more help in here?" she called.

"Stay put, Grandma," Dixie said. She shot Ed a look. "We can take care of things ourselves just fine." Ed held his face stiff as she passed.

"Fess up, son."

The stern note in his mother's voice snapped Ed to attention. The old wave of guilt rushed over him before he could think of what he'd done wrong. "Huh?" he said. Mama's eyes had a way of turning into chinks of cement. Get a grip, he ordered himself.

"What is it you're all hidin' from me?" she demanded. "And don't 'huh' me. I know somethin's goin' on."

Ed felt his eyeballs straining to look away. He shook his head and blinked. "Nothin', Mama."

Listen at me, he thought, I sound like a kid. He cleared his throat and deepened his voice. "There's nothing for you to worry about, Mama." He pushed himself up straight in the chair and looked her in the eye again. "Nothing."

Iris sighed, and as she released the air Ed thought of Sarah's tire deflating on itself as they watched. "Reckon I'm just an old woman," she muttered, and closed her eyes.

Ed felt a sudden chill even in the incredible humidity. She was gonna die.

He wiped the sweat off his temple on his shirt-sleeve. Don't, Mama, he thought suddenly. He wanted to put the air back in her. She looked empty, curled in on herself.

"Naw, Mama," Ed said. "You ain't old."

Hands folded across her stomach, head bent down, Iris rolled her eyes up to meet his. "Fess up," she said.

Ed opened his mouth then shut it. He could hear Red shouting and Sarah laughing behind him and the clatter of dishes through the screen door. A mockingbird chattered suddenly overhead then fell silent. Iris's gaze was the only alive part of her. Ed felt his headache again.

"Why don't you talk to Dixie?" The words were slow. Her mouth hardly seemed to move. "Why don't you like her friend?"

Ed wanted to blink, but he couldn't.

"Fess up, boy."

Ed struggled. I'm sixty-one years old, he reminded himself. He cleared his throat. "It's nothin' for you to worry about, Mama," he said.

Iris shook her head. "Not hearin' me again, Cap," she muttered.

Is she talkin' to Papa, Ed thought, and the chill crept up his spine again suddenly. She'd always been so clear . . .

"May's well be dead." She looked up and into space as if staring at someone not there.

"Mama?"

She continued to look up, then finally said, "You never was much fun at picnics, Cap."

Blessing the food had always meant a lot to Ed. When he was a little boy, he had listened intently to his father's prayers and had practiced different versions until he had just the right phrases and tone down. It would have been easy to fall into saying it by rote after all these years, but even though he pretty well had the right words down, he always tried to keep his spirit right in it. The Lord was always listenin' . . . He did try to come up with a new turn now and then to keep Him from gettin' bored.

"Almighty Father," he started off. That was one of his favorites. It rolled out deep and strong, like the rumble of a well-tuned diesel engine, and who wouldn't feel awful proud to be addressed in such a way? "We come before You, humble servants today —"

"Cap? Where you goin', Cap?"

What the heck? Ed faltered for a second. Mama *never* interrupted a prayer.

"We, uh, we praise Your name for the beautiful day You've given us, and uh . . ."

"Mother?" Betty's voice was soft, but dang it, this was his minute to talk to God. She knew better. Just like her singin' in the car. If they were in the car, at least he could turn up the radio. Ed deepened his voice and prayed louder. "We ask Your blessing on this food prepared by Your hand, and on —"

"Where's Granny 'n Gramma goin'?" Red piped in a stage whisper.

Ed opened his eyes and glared at the boy. What the heck? His mama was wandering off down the yard toward the goldfish pool and Betty followin' right behind. Sarah and Dixie and Melissa had turned to stare. Danged women, downright blasphemy. But Bud had a firm hand on each of his boys' shoulders, his eyes still clenched shut.

". . . And on this group gathered here before You." Ed just spat it out. "In Your name Amen."

Dix was already off after the other two. Next thing you know they'd all be walkin' out durin' the preacher's sermons. "What is going on here!" he bellowed.

144

Sarah looked hard at him. "I think your mother is hallucinating," she said.

"Aw, nothin' wrong with her," Ed said. "Just the sun." He glanced off to where Betty and Dixie were leading Mama back toward the house. It wasn't nothin', he thought, trying to convince himself. Just a spell. Buddy was almost there, offering his arm. "Betty'll take care of her. Prob'ly just tired. Just havin' a spell." He watched out of the corner of his eye. She did look pretty worn out. Kinda frail and small. Naw. She'd be fine. "Less eat, eh, boys?"

"I'll go see if there's anything I can do to help," Melissa said, hoisting the baby up and turning for the house. "Sarah, will you keep an eye on these boys for me?"

"Heck," Ed blustered, "ole grandpop will take care of these fellers, eh?" He started getting the bread for the sandwiches and some chips on paper plates. "We kin take purty good care of ourselves, huh?"

Sarah crossed her arms over her chest and rocked back on her heels, watching.

He worked at the cellophane wrapper on the slice of cheese. Red tried to tickle him, then wound around and through his legs, then fumbled at his belt.

"I'm hungry, Granpa," Skeeter whined.

"Okay, okay." Dang, that cheese wrapper wouldn't give. "Red, go on now. Let grandpa try to undo this cheese."

"Kin I cut the watermelon?" Red shouted.

"Put that knife down, now, boy!"

Ed glanced up. Sarah was standing back with her hands in her pockets, grinning.

"Need some help?" she asked.

145

Shoot, this was women's work anyway. "All right," he grumbled. "You make these boys some sandwiches, and I'll cut open that melon."

She unwrapped the cheese easily and asked Skeeter what kind of chips he wanted. Ed looked around for Red and caught sight of his blue shirt over by the crane truck. Good, he thought, keep him outa the way for a minute.

The screen door slammed and Betty and Melissa came out, Betty holding Peanut, and Melissa carrying a roll of paper towels. "Where's Red," Betty called.

Ed pretended not to hear. They never trusted him with the boys. Heck, boys could take care of themselves well enough.

"Christ!"

He heard Dixie's shout from the upstairs window and saw Sarah's head snap around to look at her. Cussin', and in front of his grandsons —

"Watch your langu —" he shouted up, forgetting that he wasn't speaking to her, but his voice was suddenly drowned out by the roar of the diesel engine. His hand reached back to his belt loop. The keys were gone. Red.

"Red!" Dang that boy! Ed turned toward the truck and saw Sarah running. "Aw," he mumbled to himself, "he cain't get it into gear or anythin'." Then the camellia bushes in front of the truck began to shake.

"Hey!" That little rascal, he thought proudly. The bumper of the semi appeared as the camellia bushes bent under the wheels. It grumbled slowly forward toward the pecan tree. Right toward him.

"Skeeter!" he heard Betty screech.

Without thinking, he grabbed the watermelon and

looked around for Skeeter, who was standing a few paces away, watching the semi roll toward him, sucking on his thumb. The truck rumbled forward.

Ed started for him. He flashed back to playing football, to Buddy playing football, and he knew neither one of them had been fast enough, even back then, to get Skeeter and get away before the truck —

The heat of the engine was like a breath in his face as he snagged the boy up. All he could hear was its slow chug, chug, chug. He saw his reflection in the bumper, melon under one arm, Skeeter, thumb still in his mouth, under the other. That look on his face. He breathed in to toss Skeeter away, and everything went silent.

The man in the chrome looked back at Ed, surprised. The mockingbird chortled above. He looked up.

Red was staring down through the windshield, eyes wide. Sarah's red hair appeared, followed by her pale face, suddenly grinning. She held up the ring of keys.

"So this is what you call a picnic," she called.

*M*y father never scored points. He was a defensive player in high school football, a guard or a tackle. It was a position of brute force. Of simply saying no. His job was to keep the other team from advancing, from scoring. To stop, squelch, shut down forward movement.

I learned quite a lot about football from my ex-husband, John. He would roll us a joint or two, and we would sit and smoke in front of the TV and he would explain football to me. I would think occasionally about writing, but instead he would roll me another joint and I'd forget what I was about to do, what I needed to say, where I needed to go.

So I learned that the defense exists to stop the other team from scoring points. It began to make sense to me that Buddy had wanted to play offense. My father would alternately deride the "glory boys" of the offense and encourage Bud to try out for offensive positions. And Bud wanted to score points. Until the second time his ankle broke, he seemed to me a running back, advancing down the field, always about to score. He was the glory boy.

So he took the bumps and bruises. One time a four-by-four dropped on his head "by accident" at Dad's construction site. He complained that he hurt his ankle in football practice and Dad said, "He's faking," and told him to "take it like a man." They discovered three years later that it had been broken and had healed badly, ending Bud's promising career as an offensive back. The scholarships crumbling away, Dad took him into the business, and put my little brother into the holes, poorly shored up holes, forever caving in. I remember watching Bud duck a twenty-foot section of pipe, Dad at the controls of the crane, and I never watched again.

It occurs to me now that we never really played as a team. Any of us. We were all our own little defenses and offenses, trying to advance, move forward, score points, or simply defend, simply shut the others down. We shifted positions, We played our game alone.

I wonder now if Dad made the offensive squad in his death. Oh yes, he came here, to this room, last month, after a long trip to Savannah, after a long

*day on the job, and lay down on the still-made bed,
and had his heart attack, and quietly died. Did he
see himself crossing the goal line, ball tucked under
one arm, scoring the winning points, the glory boy?*

Small Craft Advisory

"Aw Bud, don't do that." Bud looked up from the innards of the little motor and grinned at Melissa. "Those are the only jeans you've got with no grease spots . . . were."

Bud shrugged apologetically. "Sorry." He looked around. "Hand me that rag, honey." He wiped his hands as best he could. "Just checking it out one more time."

He put the cap back over the engine and clamped it down. He loved these little ones the best; boat engines were nearly the same as the lawn mower engines he'd started on way back in junior high. Melissa sighed, and he caught himself just about to run his hands over the back of his legs. Seemed like years since Melissa had first stood around watchin' him tinker with motors. He grinned. "You didn't much care about me gettin' my clothes dirty back when we were kids."

Melissa shook her head. "Your poor mama was the one had to wash 'em back then." She swatted him hard on the rear. "Reckon she couldn't teach you no better than I can."

Bud tried to pull his wife into a hug, but she shied back from his oily hands. "No sir. Not till you wash up." He circled an arm around her anyway and kissed her hard on the mouth.

"You 'bout done in here, boy?"

Ed squinted into the shade of the garage, and Bud saw the look of distaste his dad always had when confronted by affectionate displays. He remembered the rage Dad had flown into when he'd seen him and Melissa holding hands in church that time. Had forbade them to see each other. 'Course, I just snuck out as soon as he turned his back and proposed to her, Bud thought. Melissa wriggled to get loose, but Bud held her firm with a heavy arm, feeling smug.

"Me 'n these boys're rarin' ta go," Ed said.

"Come on," Red whined, pulling Sarah into the garage behind him. "You gotta go fishin' with us. Aunt Dixie is the bestest fisher ever. She promised yesterday she'd go. You gotta too."

Bud felt his wife tense under his arm.

"Okay, okay," Sarah said. She looked at Ed, and Bud felt a smirk well up to match hers. "Your grandpa told me he knew some really terrific fishing spots around here."

Ed looked sick. Melissa stepped from under Bud's arm. "I reckon I'll be goin' too, then," she said.

Bud looked at her, surprised. Melissa wasn't much for small boats nor Ed nor fish.

"I'll get the car," Ed said, disappearing into the sunshine again, Red following him.

"You're really going fishing?" Bud asked his wife.

She looked past him at Sarah. "I'm watching out for my boys," she said firmly.

Oh, Bud thought. She'd been furious about Dix and Sarah kissing in front of the kids. Now she was bound to keep 'em in line. Bud shook his head and pulled the tarp tighter over the boat. "Whatever," he muttered.

Bud's basic philosophy was live and let live. Oh yeah, they'd told Dix not to tell the kids she was gay, but it wasn't any big deal to him. Melissa was kinda hard on that point. Kids don't notice all that much anyway, he figured.

The two women left the dim garage at the sound of the car backing in. They avoided each other's space like a couple of cats, all prickly.

Bud sighed. This was not going to be any pleasure trip, that was for sure. No way was he gonna be stuck in a small boat with that bunch. He spent more than enough time with his dad already. Mom had tried to talk him into going along, but she understood. She worried too much anyway. The engine was perfect, and Dad and Sarah both knew how to handle a boat. 'Course, the boys... Bud wished he could get them to himself to go fishing or something now and then, but his dad, well, his dad

153

controlled the work schedule, not to mention the paychecks, and heck, the kids loved the old man. 'Course who wouldn't love somebody who let you get away with anything and bought you every toy in sight?

"Small craft advisory for later this evening —" squawked the radio news as his dad opened the car door.

"Think you ought to reconsider this trip, Dad?" Bud said.

"Nah." Ed tousled Red's hair. "We ain't gonna be out long enough to see any chop. Not a cloud in the sky."

Bud shrugged and hitched the boat trailer to the car. He was probably right. This would be a good reason to keep it short anyway. Bud yawned, thinking about the easy chair in front of the TV. Stock car races this afternoon. Yep, he'd definitely get himself some good sleep while they were out dropping hooks.

They all piled into the car, Ed and the boys in the front seat and the three women in the back, Dix separating her lover and sister-in-law. Lord help 'em, Bud thought.

"Dad," he started, "the tools and extra plugs are under the —"

The Lincoln crunched off down the drive, oblivious to him. "Take it easy if you hit any chop," he muttered to himself. Always hit the waves dead on, he thought. The dog barked, chasing the car down the drive.

*D*ad had a hunting dog when we were growing up. He didn't keep it at home, but at his construction yard in a run. He didn't want the dog to become too attached to us, a pet, a family dog. It was a hunting dog, a pointer bird dog, with a dog's friendly dopey expression and sad brown eyes and a whip-sharp tail and big orange-brown spots on white. It was Dad's hunting dog, trained in long sessions on Saturdays and after church on Sundays, trained while we stayed home, to find pretty brown birds, point them out in an eerie, quivering stillness, then flush them for Dad's shotgun.

Buddy was crazy to have a dog, but Dad said no, that he hated pet dogs, they were worthless. Mom has a lap dog now, a spaniel named Baby, just the sort Dad hated.

My dog, Dawg, sleeps under my desk in these quiet mornings, while I write. In the afternoon, he'll amble out to the cool cement of the front porch or dig a hole under the house. He slobbers and he scratches and he's worthless, but he loves me. He sighs in his sleep and twitches in dreams, and I wonder how Buddy might have been different if Dad's pointer had been his.

My dog does not hunt, except in his dreams, and I remember all those soft dead birds Dad would bring home, and I wonder if Dad's pointer would not have been happier with Bud.

The pointer was a huge space between my father and his children. We wished we were the dog, privileged with our father's time and attention and love. Perhaps he wished the same.

How to Bait a Hook

It sure was a big river. It sure took a long time to get to where the fish were. "Granpa, how come we can't catch the fish that's in this part of the water?" Red asked.

Granpa grinned, his wide red face sinking into the lines and wrinkles. "Cuz I know where the big ones are," he said.

"Good!" Red grinned back. "I ain't keepin' no little'uns!"

He looked down at the tea-colored water and the white part where the boat was cutting through the surface. Maybe if he put his hand down there he could catch a fish just when they were passing by . . . He felt a jerk on the back of his pants as he bent over.

"Paul Jefferson Major, if I have to tell you to sit down in that seat one more time —" Mama sounded like she meant it. Mad.

Red settled down and tried to watch the marsh grass island they were passing. If something happened, he could build a hut out of those weeds and live right there on that island. Fiddler crabs waved their one jumbo claw up in alarm as the waves from the boat washed up on the mud. Yeah, he could eat fiddler crabs, even though they were awful hard to catch. Or maybe fish.

"Seems like awful far to go just for an hour or two." Mama sure sounded irritated. Daddy'd pay a lot better attention when she sounded like that than Granpa would.

"Aw, I just thought we'd go across to Roses Bluff," Granpa said. "Ain't been there since I was a kid, and I know for a fact there's some mighty good fishin' there with all them trees that's fallen in over the years."

"Yeah, and we wanta catch the big ones!" Red yelled and stood up. Mama's pulling sat him down again. The wind made his hair tickle his head. He clasped his hands over his scalp to hold it down.

"The Bluff," Aunt Dix said. "That's an hour over and an hour back. And the tide against us too."

Granpa pretended not to hear her. He was always pretending like that.

Zorro put her feet up on Red's lap. "That's okay, it's sunny and I'm comfy."

Red giggled and tried to push her feet off, but she kept putting them back. "Hey!" He shoved harder. "Move 'em off a' me!" He stumbled and fell into the bottom of the boat.

"Stop it now!" Mama shouted. "It's bad enough I have to watch out for my kids in a boat in the middle of the river with him taking us hither an yon without you riling this one up more." She was looking at Zorro.

Red grabbed her hands from where they were holding Skeeter. "I'm sorry, Mama. It was my fault. We were just playin'." He didn't want her to be mad at Zorro. If she got mad at Zorro, Mama wouldn't let him play with her anymore.

Aunt Dix helped him back on his seat, and he decided to try really hard to be good. Aunt Dix and Zorro mumbled something under the roar of the motor and wind, and then Zorro started talkin' to Granpa.

"When did they say the weather was going to change?" she asked.

Red could see Granpa's eyes get skinny in the shade of his Major Construction hat. "Don't you worry 'bout nothin'," he said. "I'll take care of everything." He slung the motor smartly so that the boat cut a sharp turn into the shade. " 'Sides, we're here."

As they came slowly around the curve, the riverbank rose up so high that Red fell back on the bottom again trying to look up. "Wow," he said, and all the grownups chuckled softly. The trees at the top of the red clay bluff hung on, their roots exposed like giant spiders, and vines with shiny green leaves and little yellow flowers hung down in clumps toward the water. A gust of wind kicked by and tiny flowers spun out and into the brown river like baby helicopters. It smelled like Granny's Sunday perfume.

"Honeysuckle," Aunt Dix whispered.

They were all being real quiet now, like in church, and Red looked around for his fishing pole. He grabbed it and all the other rods clattered loudly into the bottom of the boat.

"Shhh," they all said at once.

Red rolled his eyes and sat down hard. "When are we goin' fishin'," he whined.

"You gotta be real quiet," Zorro said. "You don't want to scare the fish."

"Can they hear?" Red thought about it for a second. "They ain't got ears."

"Shore they got ears," Granpa said.

"Well, actually," Aunt Dix said, "they don't." Red looked at Granpa, who was looking grumpy, then at Aunt Dix. "They feel the sound."

"Heck," Granpa said, "all that matters is you got to be quiet."

Red started to wiggle the hook free. "Don't touch that," Mama said.

"Aw, he's fine," Granpa said.

"Like he was in the truck," Mama said back.

"Let me help." Zorro got the hook loose and held it between two fingers.

"Let him hold it," Aunt Dix said, but when he reached for it, Zorro wouldn't let go.

"I'll show him how," she said.

"Aw, let me do it," Granpa said.

"Be careful," Mama said, trying to reach around Skeeter, who just sat there on her lap, sucking on his thumb.

Their hands were all in the way, grabbing and reaching. Red could feel the hook between his fingers, kind of rusty and hard, and getting warm from his and Zorro's hands.

"Man oughta be teaching him this stuff," Granpa said.

"What!" All three of them yelled it out at the same time.

Red sat back with a sigh, still holding the hook in case Zorro let go. Skeeter's eyes were watching him still, so Red stuck out his tongue. The grownups were all yelling, using big words, and Red figured the fish were pretty well scared by now.

Skeeter slid down off Mama's lap, wove his way through the adult legs and crawled up beside Red. "Bubba," he said, and waved at the water.

Red looked back over his shoulder. The boat was drifting closer to the vines hanging down and dead trees sticking up from the river. Skeeter got up on his knees and pointed.

Granpa was leaning forward, shaking his finger and yelling. His face was awful red. Aunt Dix said, "Listen to me!" really loud, and Granpa's face got redder, but he didn't stop. Mama said, "I'm not your doormat," and Red grinned at that. Zorro was still holding the hook, and his fingers were really tired, so Red let go.

Just as he did, the boat jarred hard against something, and all the grownups toppled over the sides. Skeeter and Red looked at each other in the sudden silence. Skeeter grinned to see Red's look of surprise. Red snorted. Splashes all around the boat and then they were all calling out.

"Red, Skeeter?" Mama sounded scared.

161

"We're okay!" Red yelled.

"You stay put," she ordered.

Red looked over the side anyway. Granpa's big hand was already reaching up for the side.

Zorro's voice came from the front. "Dix?" she called. "Dix!"

Red saw Granpa's eyes open wide, and he cocked his head. "Dixie!" he yelled. Gosh, he could yell loud.

A coughing sound came from the back, far side, and then Aunt Dix's voice. "Is everyone okay?"

Red looked up from Granpa, who was squeezing his eyes tight, to see her hand appear and then her head. Mama climbed up behind her, and Zorro and Granpa afterwards.

"Catch any fish?" Red asked.

*C*hildren are a part of the Point. They are the dot dot dot, the . . . the ellipses.

My childhood here at the Point is part of the point. It is also the dot dot dot, the . . . the ellipses.

Sarah did not want children. I did. I do.

Ellipses signify something that goes on, "and so on," but they also signify something left out. What and why?

It is important.

The Big One Got Away

As the boat rocked, tiny wind waves slapped lightly on the side. The sun was warm and her T-shirt was nearly dry; Dix felt the daze of sun and water slowing the blood in her veins. She yawned.

"No napping," murmured Sarah at her shoulder. Her breath was warm and heavy through the thin cotton.

Dix shivered. She wanted to lie back, lean on the soft breast, slip along the prickles of sweat that would slick between their thighs. June in the South was like a drug. The smell of Sarah drew her, dulled inert by the heavy honeysuckle and drone of tree frogs falling in the humidity.

She sneaked a glance toward the bow. Ed and Red were looking toward the bluff, a fishing rod off each side of the pointed front, and Melissa and Skeeter were dozing, stretched along the benched sides. Her line was still and taut; the tide vibrated through the nylon under her thumb. Dix leaned back into Sarah's hand. Eyes closed, she felt the narrow fingertips trace her chin and brow. She felt the shadow as Sarah bent to kiss her.

Their lips met, soft, hesitated, then met again and parted. Dix looked up, smiled at the blue gaze, then glanced forward at the others. They remained the same.

It did not feel odd, that kiss. It was the same kiss she'd not even think about at home, away from the Point, but that life had always seemed removed from this life, this place. Something was bringing the two together. Dix closed her eyes; she couldn't get the blood to move fast enough to think about it now.

"Hey!" Red grabbed his rod tighter. "I got somethin'!" He started reeling, and Ed laughed and held the boy's belt.

"You sure do there," he laughed.

Dix and Sarah stood up to watch, and Melissa woke Skeeter.

"Big one, Bubba," Skeeter coached.

Dix felt her own line go tight. "Hey!" She looked up and Ed was reeling away too. That's the way it always happens, she thought, everything at once.

* * * * *

165

"Good mess of fish there," Ed said. "Didn't I tell you this was a good spot?"

They had pulled in five nice sea bass in a short half hour, and the clouds were thickening up. Ed pulled on the anchor. "Reckon we did near as good as the last time I was over here." He looked up at the bluff. "All by myself that time," he said. "Couldn't 'a been much bigger 'n you," he told Red.

Dix watched him priming the engine. "What happened?" she asked.

His mouth flinched, but he didn't respond. This is making me insane, Dix thought. She wanted to know the truth of that story. "Fine," she said. "Never mind."

"Yep." He acted as if he was just rambling on. "I got myself sprayed by a polecat . . . you know, a skunk," he explained. "An' Mama just went right off and left me here."

He looked at the red clay, then up at the sky. " 'Twas a day a lot like this one."

Red had leaned up closer against Melissa's leg. "Your mama left you all by yourself?" he said in awe. "Was she mean like Cinderella's mama?"

"Shoo, boy." Ed stood straight and forced a laugh. "My mama's a saint. Granny Iris is my mama. Naw, I deserved it. Done me good to think 'bout how orn'ry I'd been."

"Must of been scary," Sarah said. Dix thanked her, mentally.

"Yeah," Red echoed. His eyes were round, and he was frowning. Melissa put her hand on his shoulder, and the little body sank back toward it.

Dix wondered how it felt to have that power. She

remembered how safe it had felt to have Ed's hand on her shoulder or Mom's hand in her own.

"Yeah, well," Ed faltered. "It wasn't too bad until the rain. Pretty bad storm." He looked down the boat and seemed to hesitate when he met Dix's eyes. "Naw, I wasn't afraid at all."

"Oh, yeah," Sarah spouted out. "I don't believe that for a second. Don't believe a word of it, Red. I betcha he was as scared as you would be. Know what?" She paused, looking from Red to his grandfather and back. "I betcha he even cried."

"Nope." Ed yanked on the starter cord. "Don't you believe it, boy. I was tough. I sat right there on that bank and waited till Cap brought his shrimp boat over and picked me up. Now the wind was ahowlin' and the rain soaked me clean through... not to mention I stunk to high heaven, but I wasn't no crybaby."

The engine sputtered after the third pull, and Ed whipped the boat in a smart circle to head back out into the main channel.

Some truth, Dix thought.

"I bet he cried," Sarah said to Red.

"I think I'd like him better if he did," muttered Dix.

It was raining in hard, fat splats by the time they were halfway across. They were all, except Ed, in life jackets, and Dix could hardly see anything but the orange blobs through the rain. Damn Dad and his sentimental fishing hole, she thought, and bailed harder. The pool of water in the bottom of the boat was at least six inches deep.

The boat ran up and down the waves like a roller coaster. "Hit 'em head on," she shouted, but her father ignored her. Of course. Asshole. He'd never spent much time on the water, according to Grandma, not after the skunk incident.

Sarah grimaced and pushed past her, red hair matted down, her white T-shirt soaked to the skin. Dix couldn't help but admire the body it revealed. Her palm remembered the smooth curves. If they got out of this alive, she'd not make the mistake of forgetting it again.

Sarah knelt beside Ed. She motioned with her hands, the boat, the waves. She pointed. Dix looked forward, beyond Melissa bent over the boys, but she could see nothing but gray-brown waters, swelling up, smashing down. Lucky no one had gotten sick, she thought, looking back again.

Sarah had a life jacket in her hand. Ed was shaking his head, both hands on the tiller. Idiot, Dix thought. She found herself crawling back toward them. Maybe I'm the idiot.

The orange jacket she grabbed from Sarah was bulky and twisted around itself. Dix wedged herself behind her father, remembering him as she did so. Drenched, deaf with wind as she was, his bulk was familiar. When they were little, she had ridden him like a horsy. This, her body remembered. A wave splashed in, and they all coughed in pantomime. He seemed small. She knew his smell. Old Spice. How apropos.

Dix giggled even as she shoved him away from the engine tiller. Sarah looked at her strangely as she grabbed it, and Dix saw herself, grinning fiercely, struggling with her father who was suddenly grown small.

He struggled up, furious, and grabbed the jacket from her hands. She let go, thought he was going to slip it on, but he flung it hard, into the river, as if he hated it. Dix stared at him, marveled at the flat steel-gray hair and dripping brows. His eyes were blank, completely empty of color, like the blur of light in the storm, dead, a place to drown. Dix saw she no longer knew him. Only she would hear it, but she could not keep it in. "Dad," she said.

He looked past her, behind her, and she heard Sarah shout something. She looked around, and suddenly, right where it was supposed to be, was the Point, the white of the Episcopal Church steeple, the docks lined with shrimp boats, and the STOP sign. The STOP sign.

I stood at the STOP this morning, put my hand flat against the flat, cool metal. Red but cool. My palm remembers the cool, my eyes the red. It is the punctuation mark, the period at the end of the Point. The point of the Point.

And yet, beyond the STOP is the river, the marsh, the island, the distant bluff of the Florida side. I put the STOP behind me, walked beyond it and faced that view. The wide brown river was full to the bank, almost still, the moment of the turn of the tide. The water hesitated, swirling in on itself, slurping little waves, undecided.

This is when the fish bite, I thought, remembering. The island, the bluff, the hidden bends between marsh grasses; I have fished all those places. I have come back with what they call a mess of fish, and I have come back with nothing but a sun-dazed mind, a quiet, vacant eye.

This morning I turned back to the Point and saw the sign gray, the Point beyond receding down Main Street. There was no STOP on the river side, no red. An upside down exclamation point. No period.

Lullaby and Good Night

"Roses Bluff," Betty fumed, her palm biting into the handle of the pot she was holding. "I can't believe you did that, Ed. You knew better."

Ed's eyebrows were lowering and his face was getting red, but she didn't stop. "Out with those babies in the middle of the river in a storm. Only the Lord kept you from all being killed." She noticed she was shaking the pot at him and turned to the sink and twisted the water on with a vengeance. "Foolishness!" she muttered to herself, the rush of water covering her voice.

172

"Now just hold on a min —" Ed started.

She spun around. "Hold on, nothin'. You can be as reckless as you want with your own self, but when you go putting the lives of those babies in danger . . . Oh!" Betty grabbed the pot full of water and slammed it down on the stove a bit harder than she meant. The impact jolted her shoulder and water slopped over the rim. How could he be so stupid, she thought. "Thank the Lord, you're all okay," she said.

"Whatever," Sarah said, coming in from the stairs.

Betty whirled on her. "You! This is a Christian home, and you'll not be disrespectful to the Lord our God in this house! Is that clear, young lady?"

Sarah's mouth fell open, and she looked over to Ed, who shrugged, then looked back to Betty. "I see," she said, putting her hands deep in her pockets. " 'Scuze me."

She did look a little humbled, and Betty felt a twinge of pleasure.

"What's going on?" Dix asked, coming in from the living room.

Betty placed coffee mugs on the counter, smack, smack, smack. She felt lines in her face as thin and as hard as the marble. Her head hurt. She saw Ed open his mouth, remember, and close it like a fish in a tank. She met his eye and frowned. "Go on," she said. "Answer."

He glared at her. Just as stubborn as a mule, she thought. What if anything had happened to any of them . . .

"It appears your mother was quite worried," Sarah said.

"She wasn't the only one," Dix said. "If I believed in miracles . . ."

"You should!" Betty retorted. "What is the matter with you?" She gripped the spoon harder, then slammed it down. "What is the matter with you all? You could have been killed out there!"

They were all staring at her. Betty felt her cheeks flaming. She looked down at the hot chocolate packets. "Those children..." Her head felt like it was going to explode. The packet in her hand wouldn't tear. She took it between the fingers of both hands. "All of you..."

The packet exploded, brown powder coating her face and arms, the marble counter and floor. Betty stared. All of them. All this mess now to clean up. She looked up through the tears exploding from her head.

"What about me?" she wailed. "What would happen to me?"

I sounded like a foolish old woman, Betty thought, as she stood at the screen door looking out into the darkness of the second-floor porch, breathing the fresh damp breeze.

She slipped the latch, pushed the door open quietly and walked gently to the lone rocking chair. Be just my luck the floor boards'd give way tonight, she thought, sighing. Just as well, I reckon.

She listened to the quiet drips of rain falling from the trees onto the tin roof and the distant thunder of the storm moving south down the coast. She sat still, afraid to test the wooden floor by rocking. Guess that's what I am, a foolish old woman.

The boys were finally asleep, and Bud and Melissa were downstairs watching TV. Betty hoped Ed's snoring wouldn't bother them too much. He'd wake up sometime after midnight and come to bed, but the TV had always been his first bed. Dixie would stay up with Iris tonight. As if it hadn't been enough worrying about the fishing trip, Iris had been talking to Cap again every time she woke up. Just like he was here. Like Betty herself was invisible. Which she'd always been, more or less, she guessed.

Betty put her head back on the hardwood chair back and closed her eyes. Lord, help me lay these burdens aside, she prayed. Forgive my petty thoughts and doubts. Teach me to serve.

A mockingbird began to sing far away, maybe down at the cemetery, and Betty smiled. Sounds lonely, poor fellow, she thought. Spring's already here and gone. The summer storms have already settled into their pattern.

Downstairs, the front door squeaked open and shut softly, and she heard the rustle of someone settling down on the stoop. She recognized Dixie and Sarah in the low murmur.

"That was scary today," Dix said.

Betty didn't move at all.

"Yeah."

Raindrops staccatoed on the roof in a gust of wind. Betty wished she could see the two girls. Then she wished she hadn't thought that. Sarah's hair would glint in the streetlight glow. Dixie's arms and legs would be bare and stretched long, white.

"Why can't I touch you?" Sarah asked. "The boat . . ."

Betty wondered, confused: in front of Ed?

"I wasn't thinking," Dixie said. "You know I can't."

Silence. Were they kissing?

"I want to make love to you tonight, in this air, in this sweet, light night air." Sarah's voice was mesmerizing, soft.

Silence again. Betty felt suspended in the darkness over them.

"Don't," Dixie said. The finality in her tone, her father's, was like a rock in a pool of water.

Betty shivered without moving. She could feel the ripples wash over her, rock under her. Why?

"Don't what." Sarah's voice had tensed. "Don't love you? Don't touch you? Don't make you feel?"

Her whisper cut the air like a fishing line in the wind, weighted to the bottom. It hummed, Betty thought.

"Do you want to be numb?" Sarah asked, and Betty felt the sharp tug inside.

When Dix finally spoke, her words were deliberate, spoken, not whispered, and low. "It's better than being hurt."

Betty bit her lip and blinked into the night. So alone, that one, always so alone. The mockingbird stopped; the night went silent.

"If you don't feel, how can you love?" Sarah asked finally, very softly.

The arms of the rocking chair were rough under Betty's hands. She felt the wood crumbling into her fingertips.

Someone stood up.

"Maybe I can't," said Dix, and the door shut gently below.

*M*y mother found her first arrowhead, points, she calls them, just after Dad died. She and I were visiting the cemetery that day, carrying our rakes to tidy the family plot, speaking softly in the humid silence of midday under the oaks. Mom had grown shorter, in that way of old women, but her shoulders were straighter than I ever remembered, and she had cut her gray hair close, narrowing her face and accenting the strong, sharp lines of her cheekbones. Dad had always hated short hair on women, like my own spikey cut. Mom had gone to the beauty parlor just a month after the funeral. "I kept it long because your daddy loved it that way," she had said afterward, ruffling the soft curls on top. "This feels so good. Free and easy." She'd smiled, clearly enjoying the shade of the oaks and smell of honeysuckle vines draping the coquina wall.

I was feeling sad, dragging my rake in the dust, angry when it tangled in roots. Sarah had left me, and I was too proud to chase after her, too stubborn to tell her I was wrong. Watching my mother's form, strong though small, I felt shrunken myself, something drawn up inside.

Mom's always looked for points, always lamented her bad luck at spotting them, but she seemed unsurprised when she bent over and plucked this one from the leaves.

"Why Mom, you've found a point," I said, taking it from her, turning it over in my fingertips, a shell sharpened and thin.

The Seminoles and Cherokee both had lived here at the Point before the Spanish, and the woods are still thick with deer and small game. There are mounds on the island and on the submarine base, protected by the government now, but fishhooks and these little points made of shell are fairly common everywhere. I collected dozens in my childhood summers here.

"Yes," she said, and tossed it back into the weeds.

I stared at her in amazement. "You're not going to keep it?"

She smiled. "I'll leave it for some child to find," she explained. "It means so much more when you're young."

Mom sent me back to Sarah then. "Go find her,"

she said. "You know where." She gazed in the direction of our family plot. "I could have left your father, but I would have been no more free than you are now." She smiled at me. "Don't be too proud, too tough, to love."

Singing Fish Scales

Bud was right where she knew she'd find him: standing in the pool of spotlight cleaning fish. The tarp had already been tightened down over the boat; he'd probably checked the oil and hosed down the sides as well. This was what Melissa loved about her husband. He saw to the details of the things he loved; he cared for them.

"Hey there," he greeted her, the fillet knife in his hand raking fish scales into light-like bursts of snow.

Melissa stood and watched as he finished the scaling and held the fish down to fillet it. He grabbed another from the bucket and began to gut it. "Y'all scared the daylights outa me 'n Mom," he said. "Lotsa prayers was sent up there towards the last." He glanced up and grinned. "Reckon one or two of 'em was from you, eh?"

She smiled back. "I love you, do you know that Buddy boy?" That's what she had most wanted to live for, Melissa thought. To say that one more time to him.

"I love you too, Missy." Bud stopped and swung an arm around her and kissed her without touching his fishy hands to her slacks.

"Ew," she laughed and backed away.

Bud went back to work. "How was Dad out there?" he asked. "And Dix."

Melissa looked at the ground and shook her head. "Mean," she said. It's so hard, she thought, the silence. "Harsh."

Bud shook his head. The night was cool around them. Moths knocked against the bare bulb, and Melissa felt cozy in the circle of light with her husband. Bud set his knife down and laid the last fish on the platter. "What would you do if one of the boys was, you know, like Dix?" he asked.

Melissa looked up to meet his eyes, shadowed under his brow. "Pray," she said.

Bud nodded. "Yeah," he agreed. "But I wouldn't turn against 'im," he said. "I wouldn't hurt 'im like him 'n Dix." He paused. "You?" he asked.

Melissa thought. She would never turn from her boys, but she understood what Ed was trying to do. "It won't work," she said.

She turned on the hose so Bud could wash up. "Dixie's as in love with Sarah as anybody ever is.

Your Daddy's tryin' to make her choose between 'em, and it won't work." She held the green rubber and felt the water pulsing under her grip while Bud turned his huge hands in the spray, rinsing the scum from them. "It didn't work when my daddy and your folks tried to talk us out of gettin' married." She realized it even as she spoke. "It's the same for Dixie."

" 'N everybody knows it 'cept her," Bud concluded. He took the hose from her and began to wash the fish guts and scales from the wooden table. He glanced sideways at her as she picked up the platter of cleaned fish. "You been awful hard on her, you know, honey," he said softly.

Melissa bit her lip and nodded slowly, mesmerized by the stream of water and silver scales flying into the darkness. He was right. She'd carried it long enough. The kiss she'd seen today through the slits in her eyelids was as soft as the scaled fish on the platter. How on earth could Dix be in love, be happy, if she always had to protect herself? "I suppose I'm afraid of havin' to answer the boys' questions, of them gettin' the wrong idea, I don't know."

"The boys," Bud repeated. "Maybe it'd be better if the boys saw that we don't have to hide away. Maybe they'd be better off knowin' that no matter what, family takes care of its own." He touched her arm lightly. "That family's who you love."

He reached into the garage and switched off the spotlight. Melissa could feel his huge warmth standing still with her as the darkness softened. He draped an arm over her shoulder, and they started toward the blue television light at the back door, as if swimming with some warm Gulf Stream.

I sit here today, pushing with all my might into the place on my left hand where the thumb bone meets the index finger bone. That is the pressure point for headaches. Melissa showed me this. She studied acupressure as part of her course in massage therapy. She has a nice little business now, in a room Bud has built onto the back of their house, relieving the aches and pains of members of her church.

It hurts intensely, the pressure point. But so does the headache. My thumb digs in and the joint is all I can think about, and the harder I push, the more my headache recedes, like some tide diminishing.

Perhaps it works because it is hard to focus on two pains at once. Perhaps the two points of pain are connected.

I find it interesting that I am now willing to inflict one kind of pain on myself to relieve another. Perhaps I have lost some of my old fear of pain.

The headache is gone. I release my grip on the pressure point, and that pain recedes as well. It hardly hurt at all.

Another Saturday Night and I Ain't Got No

"You goin' to honor your Daddy's wish 'n go to church tomorra', girl?"

Dix looked up from her notebook to find Iris's eyes, steel gray and wide open, fixed on her. She was surprised. The doctor had been in while they were out on the river, and he'd told Betty to give her as many pain meds as she wanted. She'd been hallucinating all evening, Mama'd said, in and out of the drug fog. Now she seemed lucid, even bright, staring at her.

"It wouldn't hurt ya ta give in ta him this time, ya know," Iris said.

Dix thought hard for a minute, looking down at her hands, the pen. What could she say? Give in, why? He means nothing to me.

The thought of church itself gave her a chill. Whether it was the little community church where they'd grown up, where Buddy was now a deacon, where she'd gotten herself baptized over and over, thinking maybe this time it'll work, I'll be saved, I'll be saved from these dreams of girls, of women, of escape; or whether it was Grandma's white-steepled, stained-glass-windowed and nearly empty church here at the Point; or whether it was First Baptist, where Dad ushered and the TV cameras scanned the audience, and the orchestra and two-hundred-member choir scripted the service, Dix knew she'd be insulted, offended, belittled. And I am not the sinner, she thought. Why subject myself to that? "I think I'll stay here with you," she said at last.

Iris chuckled. "Why I'm gonna go to church tomorra, Dixie," she said softly. "I won't be your excuse."

Dixie met her eyes. "Oh, you're too sick for that Grandma," she protested.

Iris harumphed. "Now don't *you* go tellin' me how I feel and what I can and can't do, too, girlie." She closed her eyes for a second. "I want to be in the house of the Lord one more time before I go to meet Him."

Dix sighed. Grandma's faith was a mysterious thing. God, she'd wanted it, had tried to reach it;

186

sometimes she still wished she could reach it. But it made you as weak as it made you strong. Those black and white lines it drew were like the bars of an invisible cage. She had escaped, but most everyone she loved was still inside, and she couldn't ignore the hands reaching through, to caress, to grab. Dix looked down at the pen in her hand. Maybe that was where her faith lay now.

Iris's thin finger touched her arm and she jumped. "I'd like for you to go too," her grandma said.

Dix thought for a minute. "Well, Sarah —" she began.

"You two do everything together?" Iris asked, bluntly.

Dix felt her neck and cheeks go hot. She hesitated. "Uh, well, yes, that is . . . we do a lot together." She wouldn't lie; she'd told Mom that from the beginning. She wouldn't lie outright.

Iris looked at her oddly. "Hmmm," she said

They avoided each other's eyes in the silence that followed. A mockingbird's song spilled into the night.

"Int'resting name the boys give her, eh?" Iris said.

Dix felt her entire body go still. She barely breathed, but she could see the beat of her heart moving the white cotton of her T-shirt. She couldn't answer.

"Zorro, the gay blade," Iris said slowly.

Dix concentrated on her hands passing the pen back and forth, sweaty. If I say anything, I'll say it all, she thought. Of which am I more afraid? Silence or speech? *Love or no love,* Sarah echoed in the back of her mind.

187

Dix sighed and glanced at Iris. Her eyes were closed, the lids blue and veined, like the slightly bruised petals of a gardenia. Her heartbeat too was visible, a tired, slow pulse barely covered by paper-thin, paper-white skin. How many more beats, Dix wondered.

"I been thinkin' 'bout dyin'," Iris said suddenly, eyes still closed.

Dix sat up, startled. "Grandma," she began.

Iris opened her eyes and fixed her with the razor gray gaze. "Well, I have," she said. "It's natural. That's what you do." She paused and smiled, looking into the shadowy corner beyond the fireplace. "I been thinkin' what I learned in this old life . . . besides the practical matters, of course . . . I give you some money in my will for that danged graduate school you're so set on goin' to," she said.

Dix felt her mouth drop. "I, uh," she began, but Iris only cut her off.

"Oh, don't thank me, child, I give you the stories, I figured I'd might as well give ya the wherewithal to write 'em down proper like." She stopped and caught her breath, looked at the ceiling, and smiled. " 'Tain't much money, nohow."

Dix gripped her pen. Anything would help, she thought.

"But that ain't important anyway," Iris continued. "I been thinkin' 'bout the important things." She paused and glanced at Dix before smiling into the air again. "Like love."

Dix felt her back stiffen again. Iris too? And was she thinking about Sarah still? Dix swallowed and concentrated on no expression, no movement.

"The Good Book says, 'And now abideth faith,

hope, and love, and the greatest of these is love.' "
She turned to Dix. "I al'ays start with the Good
Book, you know." She closed her eyes again. "I
reckon I was blessed to have Cap. We had fifty-three
years, and I did love him." Her voice lowered.
"Reckon he's waitin' for me to come on home now,"
she murmured.

Dix watched her grandmother's face. It smoothed,
unfolded. Dix felt her throat tightening. She
swallowed hard again.

"I reckon most of life is about love," Iris said. Dix
put a hand gently over her grandmother's. "Cap, my
children, you all." Iris looked at Dix. "I been blessed
with love," she said. "Nothin' more important than
that."

Dix looked down and blinked her eyes clear. Iris
squeezed her hand. Is it really more important than
anything, Dix wondered. "Would you give up
everything else for love, Grandma?" Dix asked. "How
do you know when it's real? When do you know?"
She looked to Iris, and the eyes softened from metal
into fog.

Grandma laughed. "Real? Goodness child, I don't
know what that means. Real is what I can pick up
and hold in my hand. Everything else is faith and
spirit." She looked at the ceiling for a minute, then
back to Dix. "Love ain't never real, I reckon. It's
mostly just faith."

She looked at Dix for a long minute, then smiled
slowly. "Reckon that ain't enough for you, is it?" She
shook her head as Dix met her eyes. "Naw, faith
never was enough for you, was it Dixie?"

Dix shrugged. "Do you mean that love is believing
you're in love, Grandma? I don't know if that's

enough. What if the other person lies to you, or if they don't believe as strongly as you do, or if you're afraid to trust someone else that much?" Dix fingered the rough design on the bedspread. "I don't know if I can do that," she said.

Iris laughed. "Look girl," she said, and grabbed Dix's wrist in her thin hand. Dix looked at her. "You fish, don't you?" Dix nodded. Iris's eyes were mesmerizing, the fan of lines around them twitching with good humor. "Fishin' is the same as love. You can't see them under the brown water, but you believe they're there. You may have to pull out a few trash fish to get the big ones, but you keep tryin'. Same as love. You believe you're gonna catch it, and eventually you do. Funny thing is, it's the hook that brings you together, holds you together. It can hurt. It can be dangerous. But you believe."

She patted Dix's hand, released it, and closed her eyes. "Gotta have faith, believe."

Dix sat silent, looking down at the bedspread. What did this mean for her? What did it mean with Sarah? How could she ask?

She breathed in, stiffened her back, and spoke, watching her hands grip her pen. "Are you saying I ought to believe in the love I have with Sarah, Grandma?"

She heard the sheets rustle, but Dix was afraid to look up. Something cold washed over her nape, and she realized the pen was about to snap. She consciously relaxed her hands, watching the pink return to the white knuckle points, then looked up.

Iris looked puzzled. "What on earth do you mean?" she said.

Uh, oh, Dix thought.

Iris said, "I just been thinkin' 'twas time you were gettin' over John . . . near four years now . . . you ain't said a thang about no one new . . . time you was findin' a new man." Iris closed one eye and squinted at Dix. "What's that Zorro got to do with . . ."

Oh, damn, Dix thought. Now what do I say?

Iris turned her head and frowned. Dix took a deep breath of night air, honeysuckle. "Well actually," she began.

"Dixie?" Melissa stood at the doorway from the living room. She gestured with a finger. "Can I talk to you a minute?"

Iris's eyes were on the far corner of the room again. "Cap?" she murmured.

Dix stood up and watched her for a second. The gray was fogged. The lids dropped. Dix didn't know whether she was relieved or disappointed. Her stomach churned acid, the remains of an adrenaline rush.

Dix stopped at the top of the stair. It had been an exhausting day. She wondered what had caused Melissa's change of heart. Why had she volunteered to take the night shift with Iris? Her arm was still warm where Melissa had touched it, murmuring, "I'm sorry." What was that for? Dix yawned.

The house was quiet; Mom and Dad in the room across the hall to the left, the boys and Bud asleep behind the door across and to the right. A damp breeze blew in off the upstairs porch through the screen door beyond the front east room. Was Sarah sleeping? The hairs at her nape prickled.

Dix glanced to her own closed door over her right shoulder and thought of the empty bed waiting there. I want to feel her arms around me, Dix thought. I want to feel her.

The floorboards squeaked. Dix caught her breath and listened. Silence. She thought of curving around Sarah's soft hips, slowly twisted the knob, and went in.

The curtains blew inward, sheer white nylon, like ghosts. The bed was dark, rumpled, still. Dix stepped out of her jeans silently and left them on the floor. She lifted the edge of the blanket. "Sarah," she whispered.

The bed was empty.

Dix sat down on the side, her feet swinging. Gone. She was gone. Dix bit her lip. I wanted her gone, and she's gone. She hugged her knees, shivering in the night air. Even so, her chest felt empty, her eyes thick. She reached back and grabbed the pillow, stuffed it against her belly, and wrapped her arms around her legs again. Sarah's smell washed into her face.

"Damn," she whispered, and her tears shoved themselves out of her eyes. Dix dropped her face into the pillow, and smothered her sobs in the familiar perfume.

She held her jeans in one hand and the pillow under her arm as she slipped back into the hallway. Her feet were cold on the wood. The same board squeaked.

"Aha!" The door across the hall slammed open, and there stood her Dad in striped pajamas, hair standing up straight and white.

Looks like mine, Dix thought incongruously, and snickered at the thought.

"Don't you dare laugh at me, you hussy!" Ed shouted.

"Ed?" came Betty's sleepy voice from the room's interior. "What's wrong? Is something wrong?"

Dix laughed again, then tried to stuff it back down. She held her breath a second, then called, "It's okay, Mom. Dad's just playing detective."

Ed's face deepened its shade of red. "You are nothin' but a harlot, a witch, a . . . a . . . ."

"A lesbian, Dad," Dix said. "Your daughter."

"You are a child of the devil." Ed spat it out.

"You two speaking now?" Sarah asked.

Ed and Dix both spun to face Dix's bedroom door, where Sarah stood, completely nude. Dix felt the blood rush to her own face, and her head swiveled back to Ed whose mouth had fallen open. Purple rushed up his neck. Betty appeared behind him, and all color disappeared just as quickly from her face.

"Oh my," she said. Ed gurgled.

"What's goin' on . . . oh." Bud opened his door, looked out, blinked, and closed it. "It's nothin', boys," his muffled voice could be heard saying. "Just a dream."

Dix felt the giggle rupture out of her mouth, then heard it as if from someone else. She gulped and tried to swallow it back down.

Betty pulled the unresisting Ed back into their room. "I think maybe you should try to get some

193

sleep now," she said, looking over his shoulder at Dix, who was trying not to choke. "Maybe we all should."

"You lose something?" Sarah nodded toward the bedroom behind Dix. She leaned back against the frame of Dix's door, the wood dark behind the tumult of orange hair and curves of nearly translucent skin. Dix felt her hand curve to the shape of the shadow between her lover's stomach and the soft orange bush. Sarah read her mind, lifted a white hand, and stroked that favorite line of skin. She tilted her head and smiled.

Dix tossed her jeans into the room and slid her arm around Sarah's waist. Their bodies relaxed into the familiar channels and eddies of each other. Dix felt Sarah's nipples hard against her own and the long fingers stroke the backs of her thighs. They breathed each other's breath, lowered their lashes and smiled together.

"I thought you were gone," Dix said.

The blue of Sarah's eyes deepened, like the ocean suddenly dropping a fathom deeper, and she reached up and touched Dix's cheek. The palm was cool where tears had dried warm just a few minutes before. "Not yet," Sarah said.

She kissed her. Soft. Their lips barely touched, but they held them still together for a long beat. Hesitating. Like the turn of the tide, Dix thought. She cupped her hand at the bend of Sarah's waist and pulled her tight, away from the wall. Their hips nestled into each other. Dix felt the soft scratch of hair as their legs intertwined, the heat. Wet.

Dix bit Sarah's lip then kissed her hard, deep. As so often, she felt a vibration somewhere deeper than her heart, in some darker place, like an engine gunning, an animal in a den, growling, or purring. She shivered, gave in to it, and let Sarah pull her back into the room.

*C*ompasses fascinate me. So precise. North South East West. If you know exactly where you are and exactly where you want to go, all you need is a compass to find your way.

I also love maps. I have one of Point Will, circa 1843, on the wall over my desk here in the downstairs bedroom. Main Street then is right where Main Street is now, the cemetery is smaller but in the same place, and the docks are illustrated with huge schooners with sails and masts. The mill and the nuclear sub base and of course the streets on the edges of town are new, but the rest of the map I have is still accurate.

In the lower left corner of my map is a fancy compass. I look at where I am and think, if I head due East, I will go there, due West, there, due North, there, due South, there. Except that it is not that easy.

Here at the Point, you will surely need to swim, or have a boat, or find a bridge. We are surrounded, in one way or another, by water.

That last summer, before Grandma died, I felt like I was being pulled in all directions at once. All of them were murky with brown river and deep ocean and tides and currents. The strongest pull was North, and that's where I went, but there I learned that I was not metal and had no need to follow the pull of magnets. I was too cold. I had been West when I was with John, and I went East to find Sarah after Dad died. Now I have returned South. For now.

I sit here now and write and know that the compass points shift each time I move. What was East yesterday may now be West. Position is relative.

This much is certain, though. The compass always points North; I will always be looking from the South.

Sunday Go to Meetin'

"At least it's not TV church," Dix said.

She looked worried. Sarah watched her frowning through the screen door. The others had gone ahead, everyone pretending nothing had happened at all last night.

This bunch was just as crazy as Dix had made them out to be, Sarah had to admit it. Betty had tapped gently on their door this morning and called, "Up and at 'em, daylight in the swamp," and she and Dix had looked at each other and burst out laughing. Dix had shushed her, and they had listened as Betty went to the next door, tapped and called, "Sarah dear, time to get up." Sarah had yelled loudly, "Okay Betty, I heard you the first time!" Betty knew perfectly well they were both in Dix's bed. Dix had rested her head on the flat of her shoulder, and she had squeezed her hand.

After breakfast, Iris reminding Dix that she hoped to see her in the church later, Sarah had dressed, listening to the bustle of the family. The kids had yelled about things like having to wear ties and shining shoes, and Bud had been looking for matching socks, finally borrowing them from Ed; Melissa used Betty's nail polish to stop a panty hose run; Iris had to have help changing all her things to a different pocketbook. It was a friendly, happy sound, one of Dix's memories. One of Dix's stories, Sarah thought. She had waited, deliberately, until they had left to come down to find Dix.

There, at the bottom of the stairs, Dix stared out into the morning in a calf-length green skirt, silk jacket and boots, frowning. "I can't believe I let myself get talked into this," she muttered.

"Guilt is a serious motivator," Sarah said.

"Yeah," Dix said, and turned to look up. "Oh my God."

Sarah could almost see her think. Her mouth twitched. She swallowed and looked her up and down again. "Oh my God." She sat down on the bottom step and put her head in her hands.

"Well, you look great," Sarah said. She reached the lower landing and stopped to straighten her tie in the mirror. The suit was a perfect fit. She retucked her shirt into the waist of her trousers. "Don't tell me you don't like it," she said.

Dix looked back over her shoulder at her. "Oh, no," she said tiredly, "it's not that; you know you look great in men's clothes." She sighed. "Sarah, I'm just not sure I want to deal with it."

Sarah looked down at the back of the spikey white head. She squatted behind Dix on the stair and kissed her neck, then gripped her shoulders and rubbed. "You have to, Dix," she said quietly. "You have to."

They were singing some song when Sarah and Dix walked in. "Leaning, leaning, safe and secure from all alarms . . ." The crowd was standing, and a man stood at the podium . . . pulpit . . . directing the singing. A choir stood behind him. They all dragged out the syllables so it sounded a bit like they were hanging off some cliff before jumping into the rest of the line: "Lee-ea-ning."

Sarah saw one fat woman on the end of the front choir row get stuck on the "eee" when she caught sight of the two of them walking up the aisle. First she was puzzled, then her eyebrows shot up, and she clamped her mouth shut. She jammed her elbow into the robed ribs of the woman next to her and nodded toward Sarah. Various voices faltered, then restarted, as they passed row after row of suited and permed church members.

"Leaning on the everlasting arms . . ." they sang.

Sarah kept her chin high and tried not to grin. Dix's arm was tight on the inside of her elbow. As they reached the row of Majors, she saw Ed and Betty staring rigidly ahead, singing, and Bud roll his eyes, grin, then catch himself. Melissa just hoisted the baby on her lap to make room and shook her head. The little boys stared, Skeeter sucking on his thumb in puzzled concentration. Iris, sitting in the middle of the row, turned as they entered, squinted behind the standing backs, then nodded cordially. She looked forward and sang a few bars, then frowned and craned her neck back at them. The song ended and they sat down. Iris bent forward to look again.

Sarah looked around at the church as the minister prayed. The pews had slotted holders for the songbooks in the backs, and Red was busy rolling up little wads of paper to toss into the slot. Bowed heads twisted occasionally, and she would see a sneaked glance. The pulpit was fronted by a huge flower arrangement, and the preacher, a short, balding man whose vest bulged at the buttons, had a deep melodic voice. It rolled out in waves, calm and pacifying. The ceiling was very high, white walls and stained glass windows stretched a good twenty feet up. The Jesus behind the choir was open-armed, Aryan, brunette, and bland. Jesus was sort of a clean-cut American boy, Sarah thought. Some god . . . the Beave.

When the sermon started — apparently they'd missed quite a lot of the meeting — Sarah let her mind wander into the shadows near the ceiling. She was interested in the play of the stained glass on the angles, like filtered lenses. The sermon was about being a father, in honor of the day. The preacher read a selection from the Bible; everyone except Sarah and Dix and the baby scrambled to look it up in their own Bibles and read along.

"Children, obey your parents in the Lord . . ." Odd

201

that he should address children in his Father's Day message, Sarah thought. She felt Dix tense beside her. "And, ye fathers, provoke not your children to wrath, but bring them up in the nurture and admonition of the Lord."

Sarah glanced over at Ed, whose jaw was stiff, eyes nearly colorless, staring straight ahead. Then the preacher read something about servants . . . it sounded as if they were the same as children. Sarah vowed to pay better attention, but as he finished and closed his Bible, he bowed his head to pray again. She watched him begin to build steam, as if powering up an engine. "Amen," he said and paused.

"We have been studying Ephesians for some time now," he began. "These guidelines . . ." He said "guidelines" on a scale, loud then soft, lowering. He would sing his sermon, Sarah realized. He said the guidelines were on the proper behavior of Christian families. He said that children should obey their parents, honor them. He said that fathers should bring their kids up Christian. Sarah was having a difficult time not yawning. The humidity from last night's rain seemed to be gathering right where her starched collar rubbed the back of her neck under the ponytail. She ran a finger around it. Sweaty.

Then he took off. He banged on the podium, a kind of signal that he was going to embellish on the text, Sarah realized. "I am here to tell you today that the breakdown of the family is a sign of the last days," he screamed. He was sweating profusely, and he used a bright white handkerchief to smear the top of his bald spot. It made his few long strands stick up and fall over into his face. "The Christian family," he intoned, voice rising steadily, "is under attack by the forces of evil."

Evil sounded sinister, whispering up in echoes to the stained glass shadows. Sarah found herself mesmerized by the melody of crescendo and diminuendo in the little man's speech.

He crouched at the edge of the stage and pointed in a long sweep across the room. "Every one of you here *knows* what I mean," he hissed. He jumped back and paced across to the other side. "Everyone of *you* has felt the devil atuggin' at the hems of your family." He wiped his face, stepped behind the pulpit and grabbed both sides of the stand. He leaned forward. "The TV, the newspaper, the movies, the music the young people listen to is all tellin' your children it's *nat*ural to fornicate, that there's no need for the holy bonds of *mat*rimony, that Christian values are gone by the wayside."

He slipped into a jovial tone. "You know their names: the National Order a' Witches . . ." Everyone laughed. Sarah looked around, amazed. "Or whatever they call themselves . . . tellin' girls that it's okay to *kill* their babies." All around the church people murmured uh huh and Amen. "The *queers,* and that's what they are my friends, *queer,* why they're not just infiltrating our schools, but now they're tellin' us they got the *right* to be there, to be anywhere, *to come into our homes and take our children from us.*" He was shouting by the time he got to the end, punctuating each word with a fist to the pulpit.

Sarah felt a shiver as the white-haired old gentlemen in suits and perfumed women around her nodded and responded to him. She'd never seen anything like this.

The preacher said the word AIDS, and she felt Dix move. Finally. Sarah shook herself. Dix grabbed her hand, sweaty. They stood up as one person. The whole row of Majors turned their heads, and the rest of the church did the same. It was actually kind of funny, as if they had choreographed the movement. Sarah stood straight as she could, stepped into the aisle, tucked Dix's hand under her arm and headed for the door.

The preacher stopped, dead silent. Sarah heard rustling behind her, but she couldn't look, couldn't stop. She had the feeling she might be lynched at any moment. She hadn't felt this scared since the day Mama had left for good. She felt like she might faint, like the open church door was receding as fast as they advanced.

Dix's face in front of hers brought Sarah back. It loomed close as Dix reached over and grabbed her by the tie. They were right at the back of the church.

Dix pulled her in and kissed her.

"Hey, your tie's crooked, Zorro!" Red's voice echoed into the church, and Sarah thought she heard Ed's guffaw. Sarah and Dix looked back.

Red was already there, tugging at the hem of Sarah's coat. Skeeter tripped, but Bud lifted him up by the back of his belt and set him on his feet before he thought to cry. Sarah heard a few chuckles in the congregation. Melissa stopped in the middle of the aisle to hoist the baby up higher on her hip. "Red," she said in a stage whisper. "Get back here and take this here diaper bag for me."

Betty stumbled out of the pew into the aisle.

"Here, give me the baby," she said, and the two women jostled their purses and bags and the baby back and forth between them. Peanut grinned broadly for the staring congregation, opened his mouth to an O and belched in a deep baby bass. Giggles broke out around the room.

Iris gaped back over her shoulder, then whispered something to Ed. He didn't move. Betty looked back at them as she approached the doors, and sadly shook her head.

Some Father's Day, Sarah thought.

Dix's hand slipped, sweaty, from hers, and she watched her lover go back to slip an arm around her mother. They all paused at the rear door, for a last look back at the congregation.

Betty shook her head and turned to Sarah. "Welcome to our family," she said loudly.

Sarah saw Ed flinch in his pew. As they left, his head tilted down.

*W*hat exactly is beside the point? Is it all at the point? Is it all getting to the point?

Before that Sunday, Sarah would tell me that I wandered too much into things which do not really matter. That I over-analyze. That the details didn't really matter.

When I was trying to explain to her why I was afraid of her following me to graduate school, of committing myself to the relationship, she would get angry and shout, "Stick to the point!" I would talk *about my family, about the ways Mom and Dad resented each other and us, about their commitment to each other, and family, at all costs, being a straight-jacket, a commitment to insanity or unhappiness. To dysfunction. I would wonder about Bud's kids, about his relationship with Melissa. I would talk about the church, God, the rules, hopes, dreams, values. I would ramble on about the whys, the what-ifs. Why did I marry John, Mom marry Dad, Bud marry Melissa. What were the right reasons to commit. To stay. What if we changed? What if it was just the sex? What if she gave up her job to be with me and I wasn't good enough to make it work?*

"All that's beside the point!" Sarah would shout. "I love you and you love me. That's the point!"

As I stood at my STOP sign this morning and watched the sun creep between the shadows of the distant trees on the barrier island, the marshes, the river channels and banks, I considered what really is beside the Point. Water.

That summer I swam in it, went to the beach, fished in it, was nearly killed in it. Every summer at the Point, I lived with water. Grandma and Cap taught me to respect, to love it. The surface said little about what was hidden underneath. A rip tide, an undertow, could pull you farther away from land, could drag you under. A covered tree could snag your line and steal your hooks and weights, but it could also hide the big fish, the big catch, the prize. A big storm on a high tide could swallow the whole of the Point; on the ebb tide, everything, trees, lost hooks and weights, is revealed. Is all that really beside the point?

Sarah herself was outside until she came to the Point that weekend. I think maybe that Sunday she was baptized.

Sunday Dinner: A Mesh of Fish

Ed sat down heavily at the dinner table. The room was very quiet. Very hot. The tree frogs and cicadas buzzed and screamed outside. Crying for a good afternoon storm, he thought. The heads were all bowed; Skeeter, Melissa, the baby, and Betty on his left; Red, Buddy, Dixie, and Sarah on the right. Mama, on the far end, seemed crumpled, nearly asleep. How much longer could she hang on, he wondered.

They had all been here waiting, traitors, he thought, dinner on the table, silent. Mama had asked him on the way home, "Somethin' wrong with the young'uns?" He hadn't answered. He'd held her arm and walked slow, like leadin' a ghost she was so light, back to the house. She glanced up at him, hazy through the steaming food, now. "Well?" she asked. He closed his eyes.

"Lord God, almighty Father," he began.

They were holdin' hands, to keep the kids from reachin' for the food, yes, but to spite him as well, he thought. The little boys' hands in his were slippery with sweat, cold. "We come to You today askin' Your blessing on this food, this house, this famb'ly." He didn't quite trust his voice. The words came out slow and deep. Family, he thought. "Help us to be strong in Your ways, Your truth, Your word." He paused, unable to think of what to say next. His tongue carried on without him. "Lead us not into temptation, deliver us from evil, for thine is the power and the glory, forever and ever, Amen."

" 'Men,' " echoed Red, reaching for a roll.

Food began to be passed, but no one spoke, the spoons clanking against plates. Ed saw Sarah and Dixie exchange a glance. Everyone became intent on their plates.

"Mess a' fish you all caught, eh?" said Iris. She looked down the table.

"Mesh a' fish," Red repeated.

Sarah snorted to herself and glanced down the table at Ed. Her eyes sparkled and crinkled at the corners. She grinned out of the corner of her mouth and looked back at her plate.

Ed frowned to himself. Dang, if she wasn't somethin' else. Didn't anything seem to faze her.

"Roses Bluff al'ays was the best fishin' hole," Iris said.

"Your daddy proposed to me over there," Betty said.

Everyone looked at her.

"I always said I put the ring on because I was afraid it would fall into the water if I didn't," she laughed.

Ed felt himself blush.

"He told me this long story about the time he'd been left over there by himself," she continued, spooning grits into the baby's mouth.

"That English teacher at the high school had you write that down, didn't he, Ed?" Iris asked. "Never did show me that, son."

Ed swallowed. All past history. Nothin' important. His face felt hot and his collar tight. "Scribblin'," he mumbled. "Ain't worth nothin'." He focused on raking peas onto his knife. All writin' stuff down did was to cause trouble, he thought. Prob'ly what got Dixie started down the wrong path.

Red tapped his arm. "That the story you tell me, Granpa?" he asked.

Ed looked at him. The little face, nose peeling to new freckles, was empty, wondering.

"That was a good story, Granpa," Red said earnestly. Ed grinned at him. Red looked around the table. "Granpa toll me he was a big brave little boy 'n even if he did cry he weren't so much afraid as he were cold."

Dang. Ed felt his ears burning again. The rest of

the table was prob'ly lookin' at him, just like ever'body in the whole danged church'd been lookin' after they'd all walked out on him. He concentrated on the peas balanced on his knife.

"That's a nice story," Dixie said, quietly.

He lifted the knife to his mouth, watching it. No one else said anything. That's what that English teacher'd said. Nice. Good. He'd read it to the rest of the class, and the other fellas had all laughed. Nice. Ed tried to hold his hand steady, but the peas trembled just as he reached his mouth. He slurped, too late. He placed his knife gently on the rim of his plate and began to pick the peas from his lap. "Thanks, Dixie," he said softly, looking down.

"So what lit the fire under all a' you that you had to get up n' leave in the middle a' the service," Iris said.

The sounds of forks and chewing ceased. Ed looked up and found Dixie staring at him. So she had heard. Betty cleared her throat. Buddy looked down at Melissa, and Sarah looked at Betty. Dix looked down at her still fork. The boys looked at everybody else, Red sitting up on his knees to get a better angle. Iris folded her hands over her plate and waited.

"Would you look at how good Peanut is eatin' his grits," Betty said. The baby dribbled some down his bib obligingly. Sarah laughed outright, her face open and clear.

"The sermon . . ." Dix said and stopped.

Ed swallowed. Mama didn't need to know all this, he thought. "It was a fine sermon," he said, a bit too loudly.

Dix turned slowly and stared at him.

212

"I didn't care for it myself," Sarah said, calmly, and set down her fork. She looked from one end of the table to the other. She smiled at Ed.

Never blinking, holding him with her eyes, Dix put her hand over Sarah's on the table.

Iris spoke deliberately. " 'Zactly what didn't you care for about it, Miss?" she asked.

Dix turned her head to meet her grandmother's steel eyes. "Grandma," she said slowly and deliberately, "Sarah is my lover."

Iris blinked. She looked at Ed. "What do you mean," she said.

"I think what she means —" Betty began quickly.

"Mom," Dixie said softly. She glanced at her mother, then looked back to Iris. "What I mean is that I am a lesbian." She tilted her chin up, strong. "I'm one of those queers he was ranting about."

Ed felt a swelling in his chest. He watched as Sarah put her free hand at the back of Dixie's neck. She watched only her lover. Lover, Ed thought, and felt sour at the pit of his stomach. His daughter. He tried to clear his throat. Dang it, didn't they know she was too old to change? Why couldn't things stay the way they always were? His hand was tight around the knife handle again.

Mama looked at him, and he knew he was supposed to say something. She was mad. He felt his throat close. He looked down at his plate and shook his head. He couldn't.

"You are a sinner then, child," Iris said tiredly. "I won't be meetin' you in the next world."

Ed listened, and he felt Red touch his knee with a small warm hand. He looked up. Mama seemed small, and more than small, she seemed hollow.

213

"I'll pray for you, Dixie," she said, "before I go." She sighed and struggled up from her chair. "I have always found comfort in the knowledge that my children would all be gathered around me later on," she said sadly. "I done the best I could, I reckon."

Ed watched her leave, Betty at her arm, from under lowered lids. He placed his knife down slowly and took hold of the hand Red offered. It made him feel huge and wise. Sarah held Dixie's head on her shoulder, and Bud stood up to touch them before he went to hug his wife and Skeeter.

Red squirmed into Ed's sight. "Granny's made herself sad," he said, "ain't she?"

*P*oint in fact: my father, so far as I know, never cried.

Point in fact: my father, so far as I remember, never told me he loved me.

Point in fact: my father, so far as I can tell, never really hated me.

"Point in fact" was my father's favorite expression, and like mine, his "points in fact" were always *subjective. Not really fact at all, except for self. Our points in fact are fiction.*

Ed, rest his soul, was the son of a strong woman, raised on the Point, in a house of stories and rules, and I am his daughter. How much of my Point is his Point I do not know.

He haunts this room with his baseball bat and two-dollar steak and guidelines for girls, never as good as boys, except his mother, and how could that ever be reconciled? I hope his heart attack here in that bed was gentle. And I do not know why.

Point in fact: I, who knows why, love my father.

In some ways, it is Dad who brought me back to the Point this time. He left me the house in his will. He didn't tell me he was leaving it to me, but here it is, my own place at the Point.

Point in fact: There are no points in fact.

Day of Rest

"Now I lay me down to sleep, I pray the Lord my soul to keep. If I should die before I wake, I pray the Lord my soul to take." Red and Skeeter singsonged through the old stand-by, kneeling by the bed, hands clasped atop the spread.

Iris watched the small heads, one red, one brown. So small, so young, so far to go. They looked up as they finished. Such bright ones, she thought.

"Nap time, Granny," said the little one. Now what was his name?

"Okay, honey," she said. "Nighty-night."

"Ain't night," said the older boy.

He looked like kin, maybe. She couldn't think of the redheads right off, but those big ears . . .

"Ain't sleepy no how," he pouted.

A woman came in. "Even big boys need to take naps now and then," she said.

Must be the mama, Iris thought, though she couldn't place her for the life of her. "Kiss Granny so she can take her nap, now," she said.

Grandbabies, imagine that, Iris thought. They brushed her cheek barely, as boys are wont to do, but she grabbed their wrists before they could get away. "You mind your mama now, you hear," she said. They looked at her strangely and twisted their hands free. "What do you say," the mother said sternly.

"Yes ma'am," they sang in unison.

Good Southern boys, she thought, and smiled at them. Whose babies were they? She tried to think back, but she couldn't think of any of her children that had married.

Cap would know. "Cap," she called.

"There, there, Grandmother," the woman said. "You need some rest now. It's been a long day now." She plumped up the pillow and smoothed the sheet flat.

Who was this one, Iris wondered. She was right though, Iris felt plumb tuckered out. Didn't know why. Couldn't remember what she'd done.

"It *is* the day of rest, you know," the woman said.

Ah, then it'd been church wore her out. It'd always been hard gettin' all those young'uns dressed and to Sunday School on time . . . but that must not be today. They were grown now. But there had been children here.

Iris sighed. She closed her eyes. Best not to think 'bout it. Some fam'ly visitin'. Fam'ly. She dozed.

Lord, somethin' was painin' her awful in her side. Iris woke and blinked. Musta pulled somethin' liftin' one of the children or helpin' Cap yesterday on the shrimp boat or . . .

She looked around. The downstairs bedroom. Of course, Sunday nap. She yawned. The house was quiet. Why Cap musta already taken the kids down to the cemetery to rake and clean up 'round the fam'ly plot. Lettin' her sleep, that dear man. She stretched. Stiff, goodness.

She swung her legs over the side slowly. He'd go outa his mind with all that bunch to watch out for.

She stood up slowly. She'd go on down and make sure everything was okay with the young'uns.

Iris went through the bathroom to the front hall. A blazing hot afternoon, she could tell. She stepped out onto the front porch. The tree frogs was just a screamin'. There'd be a good rain this afternoon. Why, the clouds were already hangin' low and purple. Cap'd prob'ly not even notice till they was all soaked 'n havin' to run for cover. Those babies'd catch their death of cold.

She took the steps slow. Lord, wonder what I did to pain me this much, she thought. Can't remember a thing. She strolled down the road at a leisurely pace.

The moss was a beauteous thing to behold, she

thought. Hangin' down in masses of gray, like gobs of lace dancin' in the wind. Yep, it'd thunderstorm fer sure purty soon. Wind kickin' up.

She heard a mockingbird in the treetops. Happy, excited, like something he needed to tell the whole world in the next few bursts of song. She stopped to catch her breath and looked up for him. The clouds overhead were a brilliant white against the blue sky, ballooning up tall, darkening to near black farther back. She heard the first rumble somewhere off toward the east. Over the island, over the river, most likely. 'Nother twenty minutes of movin' in, she thought.

The children would hide under the beds, scared, scarin' each other more, and she 'n Cap would sneak off 'n hide in the bed. Well, maybe not on the Sabbath. Must be somethin' wrong with them she sometimes thought. Always wantin' to be together, doin' that which the Lord'd said was just for makin' more a' the family a' God. 'Twasn't bad, maybe, maybe 'twas.

Iris thought of Cap's hard, callused hands, the same hands had carried her onto the boat when she was fourteen to take her down-river, down to the Point, to be his bride. She shivered at the rough scratch of those palms on her skin, or maybe it was the wind.

The thunder rumbled closer, and Iris thought of God; did He know. Did He care?

The cemetery wall seemed awful shabby. The vines of honeysuckle and jasmine had grown thick of late. The gate hung off one of its hinges. When had it gotten so rusty, she wondered. The roots of the grass caught at her feet. She looked down and saw that she'd wore her house slippers. Wasn't that odd. She put her finger to her mouth and stared at her bare toes, the fuzzy terry cloth slip-ons now dirty.

A child's yelp brought her head up. Those kids. Prob'ly 'bout to drive Cap crazy by now. She smiled to herself. Prob'ly Eddie. The old grave-markers seemed more worn than they should be, but everything was right where it should be.

She threaded her way past the slab which covered the plague deaths . . . the list of twenty-one laid to rest in one hole. The marble angel over the Lovett plot. The gardenia bushes, not in bloom now, of course.

She walked around a huge old oak limb. It looked to have been there awhile, grass and weeds growing through the branches, but Iris couldn't place having seen it before. Nobody much cared for the fam'ly plots like they used to, the young'uns growin' up and goin' off the Point . . . Iris stopped and frowned. Something nagged at her mind. So much to keep up with . . . all this fam'ly . . .

"Mama?" The voice was Eddie's, but deep. But scared. A baby's voice began to cry.

"Eddie?" she called. Where was he? A man moved from behind a mass of rose bushes. She didn't know him. "Cap?" she called out.

Two young women, one a redhead, the other with short white standing-up hair, and a young man, maybe one of Cap's brothers, she thought, walked toward her from the direction of the family plot.

"Mother, what are you doing here," said a woman, an older woman, who tried to grab her arm.

"Who are you?" she said. "You are not my daughter." Iris looked around. "Cap, where are you?" she called. The others advanced on her. Two little boys came at a run, but they weren't her boys. "What have you done with my family," she said, suddenly afraid. Who were all of these people? They were dressed so strangely.

The light had become quite dim, purple. She felt something splat against her cheek, and she looked up. Clouds. A heavy, wispy gray shape fluttered overhead. Ghosts. A dream. "Cap," she called out, tore her arm from the old woman, and stumbled toward the family plot.

They were right behind her. Dang, her insides were aching something fierce. She wished Cap would poke her in the ribs and wake her up. She wanted to wake up. The sand was suddenly cool under her feet. Her shoes were gone. She passed the magnolia they'd planted last year. The leaves were huge, shiny, so green . . . how had it grown so tall so fast? The thunder rolled overhead. So close. Angry. "Cap?" she whispered.

She looked down. The sand of the family plot was raked into smooth neat lines and swirls, just as Cap liked it. He was here. The first fat drops splatted into the sand, ruining the patterns, before she looked up.

"Cap." She stopped and looked long at him, feeling like a schoolgirl again, all long arms and legs, and him so big and so much older. He grinned from his seat on the stone.

"Rain'll mess it all up, Cap," she said.

He shrugged and held out his hand. Iris took it, surprised at the coolness of the calluses, and knelt beside his stone.

He whispered softly, "Not all that important, anyhoo."

*I*ris was the Point for me for a long time. When she died, when we all chased after her through the cemetery, and her chasing after Cap, after love, I knew we were chasing a ghost. She was dead for me before she died.

I have here, have had for years, a needlepoint sign over my desk. It reminds me of her, straining over these tiny, tiny stitches, precisely at the time when her eyesight began to fail, to give me a message by which I might live. It says: "He who has a good point, might do well to put a cap on it."

Part Three: Monday

Let There Be Light

Dix placed her palm flat on the cool smoothness of STOP. She looked beyond the sign into the gray of morning and breathed. The air was cool off the water, scented with salt and jasmine. The sky, cool and dim, was bright only in the pinks and purples of the few wispy clouds. A fading full moon touched the distant edges of the Florida-side trees. The dark river lapped at the docks, the sea wall. She waited.

It was a week now since Iris had gone. The Point seemed not to have noticed. The street behind her was empty, the rustles of marsh and songs of early birds soothing, as always. Nothing had changed. Nothing was the same.

Dix had walked through the cemetery on her way here. She had taken the rake and created a pattern of swirls and lines in the freshly turned sand in the moonlight. The family plot had been neat for an instant, but as she had stood on the edge, admiring her work, a clump of moss had fallen heavily into her design. She had felt the urge to laugh, to cry. A mockingbird had begun to sing.

The sun pierced, in thin streams, through the trees on the island and shot yellow lights over the choppy water. It was time to go.

*T*he story is very simple. Dix comes to the Point. Iris is dying. Ed doesn't speak. Sarah arrives. They all dance in and around the Point. Iris dies. The plot points are easy to identify. The story moves along.

It is the getting to the point I am concerned with now. I am writing in this room where people go to die, watching the cardinals, listening to the mocking-birds, waiting for the next point the next point the next point.

They happen whether I move toward them or not. The getting to the point happens anyway.

And There Was Light

Dix saw her waiting beside the truck, her hair loose, gold in the first light of the morning. Sarah hefted her bag into the back and slammed the door behind the dog . . . on her way back to St. Pete. Dix listened to her own crunching footsteps up the drive.

Sarah looked up, smiled. "Beautiful morning," she said.

Dix stopped a few paces away. "You are," she said.

Sarah looked down, traced the pattern on the metal side, blushing.

"I'll call you when I get to New York," Dix said.

Sarah's hand grabbed the tailgate hard. She didn't look up. "I won't be there," she said.

Dix felt her heart grab. They hadn't talked much in the week. So much had been said, and there was too much to do: the funeral, closing up the house, and Sarah had gone back to St. Pete for a few days, "to tie up loose ends at work," she had said. Dix had called the university to register while she was gone; Dix would leave for school from the Point. They had made slow love last night. Silent. Familiar in each other's arms. They had said the words, simply, "I love you."

Dix swallowed. "I want to ask you to come with me," she said, watching her shoes sweep the gravel into lines. "But I don't know how." The shells were fragments, crushed.

Sarah's hand touched hers and Dix looked up.

The eyes were dark, the color of a calm ocean, fathoms deep. "That's why I'm coming whether you ask me or not," she said. She slipped her hand into Dix's. "No," she said as Dix opened her mouth. She placed her fingers over her lips and leaned into her breath. The familiar softness, the Sarah smell pulled Dix in. She didn't pull away.

"I'll be on my way when you call St. Pete," Sarah said finally, pulling back to smile. "I won't let you leave me behind." She walked to the truck and looked back. "You did ask, you know," she said. "Don't forget how."

Dix watched her get in the truck and pull the unruly mass of hair to her neck. She started the engine, backed parallel to Dix, leaned out, and looked around. "I don't think I'll ever forget the Point," Sarah said. She kissed Dix lightly. "It's as if it's a part of me now."

This house, Grandma's house, my house since my father left it to me, sits at a high point. From the upstairs porch, you can see glints of sun on the river. Grandma said she remembered seeing the masts of schooners from it years ago. You can see the road into town through a break in the trees as well. I am going up there in a while, to watch for Sarah.

She and I will live here now, for a while. I think I may have a child. I will name her Iris.

In the North, Sarah and I often talked about the Point, remembered the week that Grandma died. I think she learned something about family from that time. She seemed to think so. I learned she was a part of my family. Maybe she was all of my family.

She chose me that summer. She had never chosen before. She had been placed in foster home after foster home. No one had ever chosen her.

When she left for Europe last year, I didn't go. Then Dad died. He had chosen to come back to the Point. He gave me back the Point. But something was missing. Everywhere I turned, every time I climbed the stair, I hesitated at her door. So I went to find her. I chose Zorro. She is a part of the Point.

The Light
from the Darkness

Dix pulled over at the bridge, the Point behind her. The old Impala just needed to make it a few thousand miles more, she thought, north. Bud and Dad had done well by her, fixing the old car up, keeping it running these last few years. It was tacky and rusted, a hand-me-down, but the engine hummed steady, like a heart, and it was as familiar to her as this road. It had driven this way as many times as she, she supposed, and knew it just as well.

The tide was high, swirling around the pilings of the train trestle, almost still, hesitating before it turned. She watched the brown water and thought of her dream. It was the old dream, but changed.

Since she was a child, she had dreamed of the river, brown and wide, wading in it, fishing in it, crossing it on the train trestle. Always in her recurring dream, she had fallen in, or tripped, or been pulled under by a rip tide like an old woman's clawed hand. She would look down through the cracks between the black ties, become mesmerized, dizzy, and tumble over, grasping at the rails only to have them slip though her fingers. She would be wading in shallows, watching for fiddler crabs, poking in their holes with a twig, squishing the mud between her toes, and feel the current slip under her feet, grab her ankle and pull her far under and out into the deep. She would be dozing in a summer sun in the bottom of a boat, her rod resting easily in one hand, and a fish would yank her over or a storm would suddenly darken the sky and swamp the boat no matter how fast she bailed. But last night her dream had changed.

She had waded, a child; she had fished, a teenager; she had crossed the trestle, a barefoot young woman. She remembered rousing herself in the night, wrapping the sheet closer, hearing the song of a mockingbird joined by another, and then she had slipped back into the dream.

She touched the STOP, and passed it. The wind

kicked the river into a chop, and clouds were low and purpled. She walked into the river unafraid. In her dream, she swam, strong, through a hurricane, out to the sea, and she did not tire, she did not stop. She knew she would not drown.

Dix glanced in her rearview mirror. The road from the Point was empty for a second, and then a log truck labored around the curve. She flipped on the blinker and waited for it to pass. A sedan whipped out around it, and she recognized the Lincoln. Dad. He looked out as he roared over the bridge, grinned from under the brim of his Major Construction hat. He raised one finger, his pointer, in salute. Her mom beamed and waved the baby's hand. The log truck bounced the bridge as it passed, the red flag on the end popping the wind. Bud and Melissa and their boys followed it, and they too waved.

Dix smiled to herself. The Point was nothing but a puff of smoke from the mill over the trees in the rearview mirror. She pulled onto the highway and over the bridge into the lowering sun.

A few of the publications of
THE NAIAD PRESS, INC.
P.O. Box 10543 • Tallahassee, Florida 32302
Phone (904) 539-5965
Toll-Free Order Number: 1-800-533-1973
Mail orders welcome. Please include 15% postage.

NIGHT SONGS by Penny Mickelbury. 224 pp. A Gianna
Maglione Mystery. Second in a series.   ISBN 1-56280-097-3 $10.95

GETTING TO THE POINT by Teresa Stores. 256 pp. Classic
southern Lesbian novel.   ISBN 1-56280-100-7   10.95

PAINTED MOON by Karin Kallmaker. 224 pp. Delicious
Kallmaker romance.   ISBN 1-56280-075-2   9.95

THE MYSTERIOUS NAIAD edited by Katherine V. Forrest &
Barbara Grier. 320 pp. Love stories by Naiad Press authors.
     ISBN 1-56280-074-4   14.95

DAUGHTERS OF A CORAL DAWN by Katherine V. Forrest.
240 pp. Tenth Anniversay Edition.   ISBN 1-56280-104-X   10.95

BODY GUARD by Claire McNab. 208 pp. A Carol Ashton Mystery.
6th in a series.   ISBN 1-56280-073-6   9.95

CACTUS LOVE by Lee Lynch. 192 pp. Stories by the beloved
storyteller.   ISBN 1-56280-071-X   9.95

SECOND GUESS by Rose Beecham. 216 pp. An Amanda Valentine
Mystery. 2nd in a series.   ISBN 1-56280-069-8   9.95

THE SURE THING by Melissa Hartman. 208 pp. L.A. earthquake
romance.   ISBN 1-56280-078-7   9.95

A RAGE OF MAIDENS by Lauren Wright Douglas. 240 pp. A
Caitlin Reece Mystery. 6th in a series.   ISBN 1-56280-068-X   9.95

TRIPLE EXPOSURE by Jackie Calhoun. 224 pp. Romantic drama
involving many characters.   ISBN 1-56280-067-1   9.95

UP, UP AND AWAY by Catherine Ennis. 192 pp. Delightful
romance.   ISBN 1-56280-065-5   9.95

PERSONAL ADS by Robbi Sommers. 176 pp. Sizzling short
stories.   ISBN 1-56280-059-0   9.95

FLASHPOINT by Katherine V. Forrest. 256 pp. Lesbian
blockbuster!   ISBN 1-56280-043-4   22.95

CROSSWORDS by Penny Sumner. 256 pp. 2nd Victoria Cross
Mystery.   ISBN 1-56280-064-7   9.95

SWEET CHERRY WINE by Carol Schmidt. 224 pp. A novel of
suspense.   ISBN 1-56280-063-9   9.95

CERTAIN SMILES by Dorothy Tell. 160 pp. Erotic short stories.
                                             ISBN 1-56280-066-3   9.95

EDITED OUT by Lisa Haddock. 224 pp. 1st Carmen Ramirez
Mystery.   ISBN 1-56280-077-9   9.95

WEDNESDAY NIGHTS by Camarin Grae. 288 pp. Sexy
adventure.   ISBN 1-56280-060-4   10.95

SMOKEY O by Celia Cohen. 176 pp. Relationships on the
playing field.   ISBN 1-56280-057-4   9.95

KATHLEEN O'DONALD by Penny Hayes. 256 pp. Rose and
Kathleen find each other and employment in 1909 NYC.
                                             ISBN 1-56280-070-1   9.95

STAYING HOME by Elisabeth Nonas. 256 pp. Molly and Alix
want a baby . . . or do they?   ISBN 1-56280-076-0   10.95

TRUE LOVE by Jennifer Fulton. 240 pp. Six lesbians searching
for love in all the "right" places.   ISBN 1-56280-035-3   9.95

GARDENIAS WHERE THERE ARE NONE by Molleen Zanger.
176 pp. Why is Melanie inextricably drawn to the old house?
                                             ISBN 1-56280-056-6   9.95

KEEPING SECRETS by Penny Mickelbury. 208 pp. A Gianna
Maglione Mystery. First in a series.   ISBN 1-56280-052-3   9.95

THE ROMANTIC NAIAD edited by Katherine V. Forrest &
Barbara Grier. 336 pp. Love stories by Naiad Press authors.
                                             ISBN 1-56280-054-X   14.95

UNDER MY SKIN by Jaye Maiman. 336 pp. A Robin Miller
mystery. 3rd in a series.   ISBN 1-56280-049-3.   10.95

STAY TOONED by Rhonda Dicksion. 144 pp. Cartoons — 1st
collection since *Lesbian Survival Manual.* ISBN 1-56280-045-0   9.95

CAR POOL by Karin Kallmaker. 272pp. Lesbians on wheels
and then some!   ISBN 1-56280-048-5   9.95

NOT TELLING MOTHER: STORIES FROM A LIFE by Diane
Salvatore. 176 pp. Her 3rd novel.   ISBN 1-56280-044-2   9.95

GOBLIN MARKET by Lauren Wright Douglas. 240pp. A Caitlin
Reece Mystery. 5th in a series.   ISBN 1-56280-047-7   10.95

LONG GOODBYES by Nikki Baker. 256 pp. A Virginia Kelly
mystery. 3rd in a series.   ISBN 1-56280-042-6   9.95

FRIENDS AND LOVERS by Jackie Calhoun. 224 pp. Mid-western
Lesbian lives and loves.   ISBN 1-56280-041-8   10.95

THE CAT CAME BACK by Hilary Mullins. 208 pp. Highly
praised Lesbian novel.   ISBN 1-56280-040-X   9.95

BEHIND CLOSED DOORS by Robbi Sommers. 192 pp. Hot,
erotic short stories. ISBN 1-56280-039-6 9.95

CLAIRE OF THE MOON by Nicole Conn. 192 pp. See the
movie — read the book! ISBN 1-56280-038-8 10.95

SILENT HEART by Claire McNab. 192 pp. Exotic Lesbian
romance. ISBN 1-56280-036-1 10.95

HAPPY ENDINGS by Kate Brandt. 272 pp. Intimate conversations
with Lesbian authors. ISBN 1-56280-050-7 10.95

THE SPY IN QUESTION by Amanda Kyle Williams. 256 pp.
4th Madison McGuire. ISBN 1-56280-037-X 9.95

SAVING GRACE by Jennifer Fulton. 240 pp. Adventure and
romantic entanglement. ISBN 1-56280-051-5 9.95

THE YEAR SEVEN by Molleen Zanger. 208 pp. Women surviving
in a new world. ISBN 1-56280-034-5 9.95

CURIOUS WINE by Katherine V. Forrest. 176 pp. Tenth Anniver-
sary Edition. The most popular contemporary Lesbian love story.
ISBN 1-56280-053-1 10.95
     Audio Book (2 cassettes) ISBN 1-56280-105-8 16.95

CHAUTAUQUA by Catherine Ennis. 192 pp. Exciting, romantic
adventure. ISBN 1-56280-032-9 9.95

A PROPER BURIAL by Pat Welch. 192 pp. A Helen Black
mystery. 3rd in a series. ISBN 1-56280-033-7 9.95

SILVERLAKE HEAT: A Novel of Suspense by Carol Schmidt.
240 pp. Rhonda is as hot as Laney's dreams. ISBN 1-56280-031-0 9.95

LOVE, ZENA BETH by Diane Salvatore. 224 pp. The most talked
about lesbian novel of the nineties! ISBN 1-56280-030-2 10.95

A DOORYARD FULL OF FLOWERS by Isabel Miller. 160 pp.
Stories incl. 2 sequels to *Patience and Sarah.* ISBN 1-56280-029-9 9.95

MURDER BY TRADITION by Katherine V. Forrest. 288 pp. A
Kate Delafield Mystery. 4th in a series. ISBN 1-56280-002-7 9.95

THE EROTIC NAIAD edited by Katherine V. Forrest & Barbara
Grier. 224 pp. Love stories by Naiad Press authors.
ISBN 1-56280-026-4 13.95

DEAD CERTAIN by Claire McNab. 224 pp. A Carol Ashton
mystery. 5th in a series. ISBN 1-56280-027-2 9.95

CRAZY FOR LOVING by Jaye Maiman. 320 pp. A Robin Miller
mystery. 2nd in a series. ISBN 1-56280-025-6 9.95

STONEHURST by Barbara Johnson. 176 pp. Passionate regency
romance. ISBN 1-56280-024-8 9.95

INTRODUCING AMANDA VALENTINE by Rose Beecham.
256 pp. An Amanda Valentine Mystery. First in a series.
ISBN 1-56280-021-3 9.95

UNCERTAIN COMPANIONS by Robbi Sommers. 204 pp.
Steamy, erotic novel. ISBN 1-56280-017-5 9.95

A TIGER'S HEART by Lauren W. Douglas. 240 pp. A Caitlin
Reece mystery. 4th in a series. ISBN 1-56280-018-3 9.95

PAPERBACK ROMANCE by Karin Kallmaker. 256 pp. A
delicious romance. ISBN 1-56280-019-1 9.95

MORTON RIVER VALLEY by Lee Lynch. 304 pp. Lee Lynch
at her best! ISBN 1-56280-016-7 9.95

THE LAVENDER HOUSE MURDER by Nikki Baker. 224 pp.
A Virginia Kelly Mystery. 2nd in a series. ISBN 1-56280-012-4 9.95

PASSION BAY by Jennifer Fulton. 224 pp. Passionate romance,
virgin beaches, tropical skies. ISBN 1-56280-028-0 10.95

STICKS AND STONES by Jackie Calhoun. 208 pp. Contemporary
lesbian lives and loves. ISBN 1-56280-020-5 9.95

DELIA IRONFOOT by Jeane Harris. 192 pp. Adventure for Delia
and Beth in the Utah mountains. ISBN 1-56280-014-0 9.95

UNDER THE SOUTHERN CROSS by Claire McNab. 192 pp.
Romantic nights Down Under. ISBN 1-56280-011-6 9.95

GRASSY FLATS by Penny Hayes. 256 pp. Lesbian romance in
the '30s. ISBN 1-56280-010-8 9.95

A SINGULAR SPY by Amanda K. Williams. 192 pp. 3rd
Madison McGuire. ISBN 1-56280-008-6 8.95

THE END OF APRIL by Penny Sumner. 240 pp. A Victoria
Cross mystery. First in a series. ISBN 1-56280-007-8 8.95

HOUSTON TOWN by Deborah Powell. 208 pp. A Hollis
Carpenter mystery. ISBN 1-56280-006-X 8.95

KISS AND TELL by Robbi Sommers. 192 pp. Scorching stories
by the author of *Pleasures*. ISBN 1-56280-005-1 10.95

STILL WATERS by Pat Welch. 208 pp. A Helen Black mystery.
2nd in a series. ISBN 0-941483-97-5 9.95

TO LOVE AGAIN by Evelyn Kennedy. 208 pp. Wildly romantic
love story. ISBN 0-941483-85-1 9.95

IN THE GAME by Nikki Baker. 192 pp. A Virginia Kelly
mystery. First in a series. ISBN 1-56280-004-3 9.95

AVALON by Mary Jane Jones. 256 pp. A Lesbian Arthurian
romance. ISBN 0-941483-96-7 9.95

STRANDED by Camarin Grae. 320 pp. Entertaining, riveting
adventure. ISBN 0-941483-99-1 9.95

THE DAUGHTERS OF ARTEMIS by Lauren Wright Douglas.
240 pp. A Caitlin Reece mystery. 3rd in a series.
ISBN 0-941483-95-9 9.95

CLEARWATER by Catherine Ennis. 176 pp. Romantic secrets
of a small Louisiana town.   ISBN 0-941483-65-7   8.95

THE HALLELUJAH MURDERS by Dorothy Tell. 176 pp. A
Poppy Dillworth mystery. 2nd in a series.   ISBN 0-941483-88-6   8.95

SECOND CHANCE by Jackie Calhoun. 256 pp. Contemporary
Lesbian lives and loves.   ISBN 0-941483-93-2   9.95

BENEDICTION by Diane Salvatore. 272 pp. Striking, contemporary romantic novel.   ISBN 0-941483-90-8   9.95

BLACK IRIS by Jeane Harris. 192 pp. Caroline's hidden past . . .
                                              ISBN 0-941483-68-1   8.95

TOUCHWOOD by Karin Kallmaker. 240 pp. Loving, May/
December romance.   ISBN 0-941483-76-2   9.95

COP OUT by Claire McNab. 208 pp. A Carol Ashton mystery.
4th in a series.   ISBN 0-941483-84-3   9.95

THE BEVERLY MALIBU by Katherine V. Forrest. 288 pp. A
Kate Delafield Mystery. 3rd in a series.   ISBN 0-941483-48-7   10.95

THAT OLD STUDEBAKER by Lee Lynch. 272 pp. Andy's affair
with Regina and her attachment to her beloved car.
                                              ISBN 0-941483-82-7   9.95

PASSION'S LEGACY by Lori Paige. 224 pp. Sarah is swept into
the arms of Augusta Pym in this delightful historical romance.
                                              ISBN 0-941483-81-9   8.95

THE PROVIDENCE FILE by Amanda Kyle Williams. 256 pp.
Second Madison McGuire   ISBN 0-941483-92-4   8.95

I LEFT MY HEART by Jaye Maiman. 320 pp. A Robin Miller
Mystery. First in a series.   ISBN 0-941483-72-X   9.95

THE PRICE OF SALT by Patricia Highsmith (writing as Claire
Morgan). 288 pp. Classic lesbian novel, first issued in 1952 . . .
acknowledged by its author under her own, very famous, name.
                                              ISBN 1-56280-003-5   9.95

SIDE BY SIDE by Isabel Miller. 256 pp. From beloved author of
Patience and Sarah.   ISBN 0-941483-77-0   9.95

STAYING POWER: LONG TERM LESBIAN COUPLES by
Susan E. Johnson. 352 pp. Joys of coupledom. ISBN 0-941-483-75-4   14.95

SLICK by Camarin Grae. 304 pp. Exotic, erotic adventure.
                                              ISBN 0-941483-74-6   9.95

NINTH LIFE by Lauren Wright Douglas. 256 pp. A Caitlin Reece
mystery. 2nd in a series.   ISBN 0-941483-50-9   8.95

PLAYERS by Robbi Sommers. 192 pp. Sizzling, erotic novel.
                                              ISBN 0-941483-73-8   9.95

MURDER AT RED ROOK RANCH by Dorothy Tell. 224 pp.
A Poppy Dillworth mystery. 1st in a series.   ISBN 0-941483-80-0   8.95

LESBIAN SURVIVAL MANUAL by Rhonda Dicksion. 112 pp. Cartoons! ISBN 0-941483-71-1   8.95

A ROOM FULL OF WOMEN by Elisabeth Nonas. 256 pp. Contemporary Lesbian lives. ISBN 0-941483-69-X   9.95

THEME FOR DIVERSE INSTRUMENTS by Jane Rule. 208 pp. Powerful romantic lesbian stories. ISBN 0-941483-63-0   8.95

CLUB 12 by Amanda Kyle Williams. 288 pp. Espionage thriller featuring a lesbian agent! ISBN 0-941483-64-9   8.95

DEATH DOWN UNDER by Claire McNab. 240 pp. A Carol Ashton mystery. 3rd in a series. ISBN 0-941483-39-8   9.95

MONTANA FEATHERS by Penny Hayes. 256 pp. Vivian and Elizabeth find love in frontier Montana. ISBN 0-941483-61-4   8.95

LIFESTYLES by Jackie Calhoun. 224 pp. Contemporary Lesbian lives and loves. ISBN 0-941483-57-6   9.95

WILDERNESS TREK by Dorothy Tell. 192 pp. Six women on vacation learning ''new'' skills. ISBN 0-941483-60-6   8.95

MURDER BY THE BOOK by Pat Welch. 256 pp. A Helen Black Mystery. First in a series. ISBN 0-941483-59-2   9.95

THERE'S SOMETHING I'VE BEEN MEANING TO TELL YOU Ed. by Loralee MacPike. 288 pp. Gay men and lesbians coming out to their children. ISBN 0-941483-44-4   9.95

LIFTING BELLY by Gertrude Stein. Ed. by Rebecca Mark. 104 pp. Erotic poetry. ISBN 0-941483-51-7   8.95

AFTER THE FIRE by Jane Rule. 256 pp. Warm, human novel by this incomparable author. ISBN 0-941483-45-2   8.95

THREE WOMEN by March Hastings. 232 pp. Golden oldie. A triangle among wealthy sophisticates. ISBN 0-941483-43-6   8.95

PLEASURES by Robbi Sommers. 204 pp. Unprecedented eroticism. ISBN 0-941483-49-5   8.95

EDGEWISE by Camarin Grae. 372 pp. Spellbinding adventure. ISBN 0-941483-19-3   9.95

FATAL REUNION by Claire McNab. 224 pp. A Carol Ashton mystery. 2nd in a series. ISBN 0-941483-40-1   8.95

IN EVERY PORT by Karin Kallmaker. 228 pp. Jessica's sexy, adventuresome travels. ISBN 0-941483-37-7   9.95

OF LOVE AND GLORY by Evelyn Kennedy. 192 pp. Exciting WWII romance. ISBN 0-941483-32-0   8.95

CLICKING STONES by Nancy Tyler Glenn. 288 pp. Love transcending time. ISBN 0-941483-31-2   9.95

SOUTH OF THE LINE by Catherine Ennis. 216 pp. Civil War adventure. ISBN 0-941483-29-0   8.95

WOMAN PLUS WOMAN by Dolores Klaich. 300 pp. Supurb
Lesbian overview.   ISBN 0-941483-28-2   9.95

THE FINER GRAIN by Denise Ohio. 216 pp. Brilliant young
college lesbian novel.   ISBN 0-941483-11-8   8.95

OCTOBER OBSESSION by Meredith More. Josie's rich, secret
Lesbian life.   ISBN 0-941483-18-5   8.95

BEFORE STONEWALL: THE MAKING OF A GAY AND
LESBIAN COMMUNITY by Andrea Weiss & Greta Schiller.
96 pp., 25 illus.   ISBN 0-941483-20-7   7.95

OSTEN'S BAY by Zenobia N. Vole. 204 pp. Sizzling adventure
romance set on Bonaire.   ISBN 0-941483-15-0   8.95

LESSONS IN MURDER by Claire McNab. 216 pp. A Carol
Ashton mystery. First in a series.   ISBN 0-941483-14-2   9.95

YELLOWTHROAT by Penny Hayes. 240 pp. Margarita, bandit,
kidnaps Julia.   ISBN 0-941483-10-X   8.95

SAPPHISTRY: THE BOOK OF LESBIAN SEXUALITY by
Pat Califia. 3d edition, revised. 208 pp. ISBN 0-941483-24-X   10.95

CHERISHED LOVE by Evelyn Kennedy. 192 pp. Erotic Lesbian
love story.   ISBN 0-941483-08-8   9.95

THE SECRET IN THE BIRD by Camarin Grae. 312 pp. Striking,
psychological suspense novel.   ISBN 0-941483-05-3   8.95

TO THE LIGHTNING by Catherine Ennis. 208 pp. Romantic
Lesbian 'Robinson Crusoe' adventure.   ISBN 0-941483-06-1   8.95

DREAMS AND SWORDS by Katherine V. Forrest. 192 pp.
Romantic, erotic, imaginative stories.   ISBN 0-941483-03-7   8.95

MEMORY BOARD by Jane Rule. 336 pp. Memorable novel
about an aging Lesbian couple.   ISBN 0-941483-02-9   10.95

THE ALWAYS ANONYMOUS BEAST by Lauren Wright Douglas.
224 pp. A Caitlin Reece mystery. First in a series.
                                           ISBN 0-941483-04-5   8.95

PARENTS MATTER by Ann Muller. 240 pp. Parents' relationships with Lesbian daughters and gay sons. ISBN 0-930044-91-6   9.95

THE BLACK AND WHITE OF IT by Ann Allen Shockley.
144 pp. Short stories.   ISBN 0-930044-96-7   7.95

SAY JESUS AND COME TO ME by Ann Allen Shockley. 288
pp. Contemporary romance.   ISBN 0-930044-98-3   8.95

MURDER AT THE NIGHTWOOD BAR by Katherine V. Forrest.
240 pp. A Kate Delafield mystery. Second in a series.
                                           ISBN 0-930044-92-4   10.95

WINGED DANCER by Camarin Grae. 228 pp. Erotic Lesbian
adventure story.   ISBN 0-930044-88-6   8.95

PAZ by Camarin Grae. 336 pp. Romantic Lesbian adventurer
with the power to change the world.   ISBN 0-930044-89-4   8.95

SOUL SNATCHER by Camarin Grae. 224 pp. A puzzle, an
adventure, a mystery — Lesbian romance.   ISBN 0-930044-90-8   8.95

THE LOVE OF GOOD WOMEN by Isabel Miller. 224 pp.
Long-awaited new novel by the author of the beloved *Patience
and Sarah*.   ISBN 0-930044-81-9   8.95

THE HOUSE AT PELHAM FALLS by Brenda Weathers. 240
pp. Suspenseful Lesbian ghost story.   ISBN 0-930044-79-7   7.95

HOME IN YOUR HANDS by Lee Lynch. 240 pp. More stories
from the author of *Old Dyke Tales*.   ISBN 0-930044-80-0   7.95

PEMBROKE PARK by Michelle Martin. 256 pp. Derring-do
and daring romance in Regency England.   ISBN 0-930044-77-0   7.95

THE LONG TRAIL by Penny Hayes. 248 pp. Vivid adventures
of two women in love in the old west.   ISBN 0-930044-76-2   8.95

AN EMERGENCE OF GREEN by Katherine V. Forrest. 288
pp. Powerful novel of sexual discovery.   ISBN 0-930044-69-X   9.95

THE LESBIAN PERIODICALS INDEX edited by Claire Potter.
432 pp. Author & subject index.   ISBN 0-930044-74-6   12.95

DESERT OF THE HEART by Jane Rule. 224 pp. A classic;
basis for the movie *Desert Hearts*.   ISBN 0-930044-73-8   10.95

TORCHLIGHT TO VALHALLA by Gale Wilhelm. 128 pp.
Classic novel by a great Lesbian writer.   ISBN 0-930044-68-1   7.95

LESBIAN NUNS: BREAKING SILENCE edited by Rosemary
Curb and Nancy Manahan. 432 pp. Unprecedented autobiographies
of religious life.   ISBN 0-930044-62-2   9.95

THE SWASHBUCKLER by Lee Lynch. 288 pp. Colorful novel
set in Greenwich Village in the sixties.   ISBN 0-930044-66-5   8.95

SEX VARIANT WOMEN IN LITERATURE by Jeannette
Howard Foster. 448 pp. Literary history.   ISBN 0-930044-65-7   8.95

A HOT-EYED MODERATE by Jane Rule. 252 pp. Hard-hitting
essays on gay life; writing; art.   ISBN 0-930044-57-6   7.95

AMATEUR CITY by Katherine V. Forrest. 224 pp. A Kate
Delafield mystery. First in a series.   ISBN 0-930044-55-X   10.95

THE SOPHIE HOROWITZ STORY by Sarah Schulman. 176 pp.
Engaging novel of madcap intrigue.   ISBN 0-930044-54-1   7.95

THE YOUNG IN ONE ANOTHER'S ARMS by Jane Rule.
224 pp. Classic Jane Rule.   ISBN 0-930044-53-3   9.95

OLD DYKE TALES by Lee Lynch. 224 pp. Extraordinary stories
of our diverse Lesbian lives.   ISBN 0-930044-51-7   8.95

AGAINST THE SEASON by Jane Rule. 224 pp. Luminous,
complex novel of interrelationships.   ISBN 0-930044-48-7   8.95

LOVERS IN THE PRESENT AFTERNOON by Kathleen Fleming. 288 pp. A novel about recovery and growth.   ISBN 0-930044-46-0   8.95

TOOTHPICK HOUSE by Lee Lynch. 264 pp. Love between two Lesbians of different classes.   ISBN 0-930044-45-2   7.95

CONTRACT WITH THE WORLD by Jane Rule. 340 pp. Powerful, panoramic novel of gay life.   ISBN 0-930044-28-2   9.95

THIS IS NOT FOR YOU by Jane Rule. 284 pp. A letter to a beloved is also an intricate novel.   ISBN 0-930044-25-8   8.95

OUTLANDER by Jane Rule. 207 pp. Short stories and essays by one of our finest writers.   ISBN 0-930044-17-7   8.95

ODD GIRL OUT by Ann Bannon.   ISBN 0-930044-83-5   5.95
I AM A WOMAN 84-3; WOMEN IN THE SHADOWS 85-1;   each
JOURNEY TO A WOMAN 86-X; BEEBO BRINKER 87-8. Golden oldies about life in Greenwich Village.

JOURNEY TO FULFILLMENT, A WORLD WITHOUT MEN, and   3.95
RETURN TO LESBOS. All by Valerie Taylor   each

These are just a few of the many Naiad Press titles — we are the oldest and largest lesbian/feminist publishing company in the world. Please request a complete catalog. We offer personal service; we encourage and welcome direct mail orders from individuals who have limited access to bookstores carrying our publications.